TELL SACKETT'S CHALLENGE

Shanty had a nice smile. "We've got you," he said. "There's no way you can get away."

I smiled back at him. "Then take me," I said. "I'm here."

Shanty hesitated. It worried him that I was not afraid. "You came," he admitted. "I never thought you'd make it."

"There are two more up on the mountain and by now they're beginning to miss me. They're getting lonely on the mountain, Shanty, and they'll come down."

"We will handle them."

"And there are more of us where we came from. Be smart, Shanty. Cash in your chips while you still can."

He laughed. "You know, Sackett, I like you. I'm going to hate to kill you."

BENDIGO SHAFTER
BORDEN CHANTRY
BOWDRIE
BOWDRIE'S LAW
BRIONNE
THE BROKEN GUN
BUCKSKIN RUN
THE BURNING HILLS
THE CALIFORNIOS
CALLAGHEN
CATLOW
CHANCY
THE CHEROKEE TRAIL
COMSTOCK LODE
CONAGHER
CROSSFIRE TRAIL
DARK CANYON
DOWN THE LONG HILLS
THE EMPTY LAND
FAIR BLOWS THE WIND
FALLON
THE FERGUSON RIFLE
THE FIRST FAST DRAW
FLINT
FRONTIER
GUNS OF THE TIMBERLANDS
HANGING WOMAN CREEK
HELLER WITH A GUN
THE HIGH GRADERS
HIGH LONESOME
THE HILLS OF HOMICIDE
HONDO
HOW THE WEST WAS WON
THE IRON MARSHAL
THE KEY-LOCK MAN
KID RODELO
KILKENNY
KILLOE

KILRONE
KIOWA TRAIL
LAW OF THE DESERT BORN
THE LONESOME GODS
THE MAN CALLED NOON
THE MAN FROM SKIBBEREEN
MATAGORDA
MILO TALON
THE MOUNTAIN VALLEY WAR
NORTH TO THE RAILS
OVER ON THE DRY SIDE
PASSIN' THROUGH
THE PROVING TRAIL
THE QUICK AND THE DEAD
RADIGAN
REILLY'S LUCK
THE RIDER OF LOST CREEK
RIVERS WEST
THE SHADOW RIDERS
SHALAKO
SHOWDOWN AT YELLOW
  BUTTE
SILVER CANYON
SITKA
SON OF A WANTED MAN
THE STRONG SHALL LIVE
TAGGART
TO TAME A LAND
TUCKER
UNDER THE SWEETWATER
  RIM
UTAH BLAINE
THE WALKING DRUM
WAR PARTY
WESTWARD THE TIDE
WHERE THE LONG GRASS
  BLOWS
YONDERING

Sackett Titles by
Louis L'Amour

LONELY ON THE MOUNTAIN

Louis L'Amour

BANTAM BOOKS

TORONTO • NEW YORK • LONDON • SYDNEY • AUCKLAND

LONELY ON THE MOUNTAIN
A Bantam Book / November 1980

2nd printing . November 1980	6th printing . . . . . . July 1982
3rd printing . . . January 1981	7th printing . . . . . . June 1983
4th printing . . . . . . May 1981	8th printing . . December 1983
5th printing . November 1981	9th printing . . September 1984
10th printing . . . June 1986	

ISBN 0-553-25513-4

Published simultaneously in the United States and Canada

Bantam Books are published by Bantam Books, Inc. Its trademark, consisting of the words "Bantam Books" and the por-
trayal of a rooster, is Registered in U.S. Patent and Trademark
Office and in other countries. Marca Registrada. Bantam
Books, Inc., 666 Fifth Avenue, New York, New York 10103.

PRINTED IN THE UNITED STATES OF AMERICA

KR   18 17 16 15 14 13 12 11 10

To Lou Satz

Author's Note

The story of Louis Riel and the *Metis,* barely touched upon in this book, is one of the most exciting in Canadian history. At the present time, I have a book in its development stages which will deal with this subject at greater length, and touch upon some other aspects of Western Canadian history.

Early travelers in Western Canada had much to say about the mosquitoes and these stories in this book are not exaggerated. David Thompson, Palliser, the Earl of Southesk, Butler, Traill, Kootenai Brown and many others told such stories as those repeated here.

—*Louis L'Amour*

Chapter I

There will come a time when you believe everything is finished. That will be the beginning.

Pa said that when I was a boy. There was a hot, dry wind moaning through the hot, dry trees, and we were scared of fire in the woods, knowing that if fire came, all we had would go.

We had crops in the ground, but there'd been no rain for weeks. We were scrapin' the bottom of the barrel for flour and drinkin' coffee made from ground-up beans. We'd had our best cow die, and the rest was ganted up, so's you could count every rib.

Two years before, pa had set us to diggin' a well. "Pa?" I asked. "Why dig a well? We've got the creek yonder and three flowin' springs on the place. It's needless work."

He lifted his head, and he looked me right in the eye and said, "Dig a well."

We dug a well.

We grumbled, but when pa said dig, you just naturally dug. And lucky it was, too.

For there came the time when the bed of the creek was dust and the springs that had always flowed weren't flowin'. We had water, though. We had water from a deep, cold well. We watered our stock, we watered our kitchen garden, and we had what was needful for drinkin' because of that well.

Now, years later and far out on the grass prairie, I was remembering and wondering what I could do that I hadn't done.

1

No matter which way you looked between you and anywhere else, there was a thousand miles of grass—and the Sioux.

The Sioux hadn't come upon us yet, but they were about, and every man-jack of us knew it. It could be they hadn't cut our sign yet, but cut it they would, and when they did, they would come for us.

We were seven men, including the Chinese cook, in no shape to fight off a bunch of Sioux warriors if they came upon us. Scattered around the cattle, we'd be in no shape at all.

"If it comes," I told them, "center on me and we'll kill enough cattle for a fort and make a stand."

Have you seen that Dakota country? It varies some, but it's likely to be flat or low, rolling hills, with here and there a slough. You don't find natural places to fort. The buffalo wallows offer the best chance if there's one handy. The trouble was, if the Sioux came upon us, it would be a spot of their choosing, not ours.

The buffalo-chip fire had burned down to a sullen red glow by the time Tyrel rode back into camp. He stripped the gear from his mount and carried his saddle up to the fire for a pillow. He took off his chaps, glancing over at me, knowing I was awake.

"They're quiet, Tell"—he spoke soft so's not to wake the others, who were needful of sleep—"but every one of them is awake."

"There's something out there. Some*thing* or some-*body*."

"This here is Injun country." Tyrel shucked his gun belt and placed it handy to his bed. He sat down to pull off his boots. "We knew that before we started."

He went to the blackened, beat-up coffee pot and looked over at me. "Toss me your cup."

Well, I wasn't sleeping, nohow. I sat up and took the coffee. "It ain't Injuns," I said. "Least it doesn't *feel* like Injuns. This is something else. We've been followed, Tyrel. You know that as well as me. We've been followed for the last three or four days."

2

The coffee was strong enough to grow hair on a saddle. "Tye? You recall the time pa wanted us to dig that well? He was always one to be ready for whatever might come. Not that he went around expecting trouble. He just wanted to be ready for whatever happened. For anything."

"That was him, alright."

"Tyrel, something tells me I forgot to dig my well. There's something I should have done that I've missed, something we've got to think of or plan for."

Tyrel, he just sipped his coffee, squatting there in his sock feet, feeling good to have his boots off. "Don't know what it could be," Tyrel said. "We've got rifles all around and ammunition to fight a war. At Fort Garry, Orrin will pick up some Red River carts and a man or two. He'll load those carts with grub and such." He pushed his hat back, sweat-wet hair plastered against his forehead. "The stock are fat—eleven hundred head of good beef, and we've gotten an early start."

"Don't make no difference, Tyrel. I've forgotten something, or somebody."

"Wait'll we meet up with Orrin. When he joins us at Fort Garry, he'll know right away if anything's wrong."

"I've been thinkin' about Fort Garry, Tyrel. Seems foolish to drive east even a little way when we've got to go back west."

Tyrel refilled his cup and held up the pot. I shook my head. "It's the boys," he said. "This here shapes up to be a rough, mean drive. Oh, we'll see some new country, an' mighty beautiful country, but any way you take it, it will be rough. We'd better give the boys a chance to blow off some steam."

"They'd better blow it careful," I said. "Some of those Canadians are mighty rough. Nice folks, but they can handle themselves."

Low clouds blotted out the stars; wind whispered in the grass. Sleep was needed, but I was wakeful as a

3

man with three sparklin'-age daughters. "You were there when the word came, Tyrel. D'you figure there's more to this than Logan let on?"

"You know Logan better'n I do. He cut his stick for trouble before he was knee-high to a short hog, and you know any time Logan calls for help, there's no telling what's involved. There's mighty little in the way of trouble Logan can't handle all by himself."

"He never lied to us."

"He never lied to nobody. Nolan and Logan have done things here and there that you and me wouldn't, but they never broke their given word."

Tyrel bedded down, but I lay awake, trying to think it out, tired though I was.

We were pushing eleven hundred head of fat steers across the Dakota plains, headed for the gold mines in far western Canada. The Dakota country was new to us. Wide, wide plains but good grass so far, and we'd been lucky enough to come upon water when needed. Cap Rountree had been up this way before, but aside from Tyrel, who had been marshal of a gold-minin' town in Idaho, none of us had been so far north.

We'd put the herd together in a hurry because Logan was in need and started the drive short-handed, which meant extra work for all. Orrin was coming up by steamboat and was to meet us at Fort Garry for the long drive west.

Those to whom we'd talked, who might or might not know what they were talkin' about, said there were no towns to the west. There were trading posts here and yonder, however, one of them being Fort Whoop-Up.

Even about that we heard two stories. Some said it was simply a trading post, but others said it was a hangout for rustlers, whiskey peddlers, and the like. If it was kin to such places as we'd known, it could be both.

We Sacketts had come west from the Tennessee-North Carolina country in search of new lands. Ours had been among the earliest folk to settle back yonder,

4

but somehow we stuck to the high-up hills where the game was and let the good bottom lands slip away to latecomers. Most newcomers to the west found the life hard and the ways rough, but to mountain-bred folks it was no different from what we were accustomed to.

Any time a Sackett had meat on the table, it was likely to be meat he'd shot, and if pa was away from home, it was we youngsters who did the shootin'. Those who lived 'round about used to say that Sacketts and shootin' went together like hog meat an' hominy.

Stock driving had been our way of life since first we settled in the hills. It was old Yance Sackett who began it some two hundred years back, and he started it with turkey drives to market. After that, it was hogs, and, like turkeys, we drove them afoot, for the most part.

If you had turkeys or hogs to sell, you just naturally drove them to market or sold them to a drover.

Word came from Logan just after we'd sold nine hundred head of prime beef in Kansas. We'd actually sold fourteen hundred head, but some of the stock belonged to neighbors.

Cap Rountree, Tyrel, and I were at a table in the Drover's Cottage when that man with the green eye-shade came up to me and said, "Mr. Sackett? This here message come for you a day or two back. I reckon it's important, and I just now heard you were in town."

"Cap," I said, "if you and Tyrel will pardon me, I'll just see what this is."

"Shall I read it?" Tyrel asked me.

"You might," I said, and was glad for the offer. When it came to schoolin', I'd come up empty, and whilst I was learning to read and write, I was mighty short on words. There were still a good many I'd never driven into the corral to slap the brand of memory on.

Tyrel had only learned to read a short time back, but he could read handwritin' as easy as print, nigh as good as any schoolmarm.

He opened up that message like he'd been gettin' 'em

every day. He looked over it at me. "Listen to this," he said.

William Tell Sackett,
Drover's Cottage,
Abilene, Kansas.

I taken money to deliver several hundred head of beef cattle before winter sets in. I got no cows. I got no money. I can't get away to help. Withouten they get them cows, folks will starve, and I'll be wearin' a rope necktie.

Logan

P.S. You can expect Higginses.

"Higginses?" Cap said. "I thought you'd done rolled up their carpet?"

"By 'Higginses' he means we can expect trouble. For some reason he didn't want to say that, but he knew we'd understand."

"Those Higgins boys were rough," Tyrel said, "and we sure didn't dust off all of them. They were good folks, only we just didn't get along."

"Fact is," he added, "there was one of those Higgins gals who used to give me the big eye back yonder in school. *Boy, was she something!* She'd give me a look out'n those big blue eyes, and I wouldn't know come hither to go yonder."

Cap, he was a-settin' there lookin' at me out of those wise old eyes. "He wants beef cattle, and we've just sold our stock. We got a piece of money, but we ain't got near enough to buy at these prices. So what do we do?"

"We've got to buy," I said.

"We haven't got enough to buy, let alone to feed ourselves from here to Canada. It's a far piece."

Whilst we ate, I did some studyin'. The thought of not doing it never entered our minds. We Sacketts just naturally stood by one another, and if Logan was in trouble, we'd help. Undoubtedly, he'd given his word to deliver cattle, and a Sackett's word was his bond. It was even more than that. Anywhere a Sackett was known, his name was good for cash in the hand.

This was going to take every cent we could put our hands on, and worst of all, we had to *move!*

Cap put down his cup. "Got me an idea," he said, and was gone from the table.

"This couldn't come at a worse time," Tyrel commented. "I need all I've got to pay debts back in Santa Fe."

"Me, too," I said, "but Logan's in trouble."

"You believe he meant that about hanging?"

"Logan is a man who takes hanging right serious, and he wouldn't joke about it. If he says hanging, he means just that." For a moment there, I paused, looking into my coffee. "From that remark about Higginses, we can expect trouble along the way."

"Sounds like Logan figures somebody doesn't want the cattle to get through"—Tyrel glanced over at me—"which doesn't make a lot of sense."

Cap was coming back into the room followed by a straw-hatted sod buster wearing shoes. Farmers were beginning to settle around, but a man didn't see many of them yet, and almost never in the Drover's Cottage.

"Set, Bob, an' tell them what you told me," Cap said.

Bob had wrinkles from squinting at the sun and wrinkles around his eyes from laughing. "My cousin's come down from the north. Lives up on the Missouri near Yankton. He was telling me about some Indian cattle, and Cap here, he overheard us."

"Indian cattle?"

"Well, some of them. Quite a few years back, two brothers brought some cattle into the Missouri River country. One of the brothers was gored by a steer, and by the time the other one found him, he was in bad shape. Blood poison, or whatever. He lasted a few weeks, then died.

"The brother took the body back home for burial, and when he came back, he was crossing a stream when his horse fell with him. Both of them lost—horse and man.

"So those cattle run wild. The Injuns around there are mostly friendlies, and they killed a steer time to time, but those cattle have run wild in some of the gullies leading back from the river. I'd say if anybody has claim on them now, it's those Injuns."

"But would they sell them?"

"Right now they would. They'd sell, and quick. You see, the Sioux have been raiding into their country some, and just now the Sioux learned about those cattle. They'll drive them off, leaving the friendlies with nothing. If you were to go in there and make 'em a decent offer, you'd have yourself a herd."

"How many head, do you figure?"

"Eight, nine hundred. Maybe more. There's good grass in those bottoms, and they've done right well. What you'll find is mostly young stuff—unbranded. What Texas folk call mavericks."

So that was how it began. We met the Injuns and sat down over a mess of bacon, bread, and beans, and we made our deal. They didn't want the Sioux to run off those cattle, and we paid them well in blankets and things they were needing.

There was a star showing here and there when I rolled out of my blankets and shook out my boots. The morning was cold, so I got into my vest and coat as quick as ever I could, and after rolling my bed, I headed for the cook fire and a cup of coffee.

Lin, our Chinese cook, was squatting over the fire. He gestured to the pot. "All ready," he said.

He dished up a plate of beef and beans for me, and when I'd taken a couple of swallows of coffee, almost too hot to drink, I started on the beans.

"These are good. What've you done to them?"

"Wild onions," he said.

My eyes swept the horizon. Far off to the west, I

could see some black humps. "Buffalo," I commented.

He stood up to look. "I have never seen a buffalo. There will be more?"

"A-plenty. More'n we want, I expect."

Leaving the fire, I saddled up and then returned for another plate of the beef and beans. When a man rides out in the morning on a cattle drive, he never knows when he will eat again. Too many things can come up.

Whether it was the wild onions, I did not know, but his grub was the best I'd ever tasted in a cow camp. I told him so.

"I've never cooked but for myself." He glanced at me. "I go home now, to China."

"Isn't this the long way?"

"You go to British Columbia? I have a relative there, and ships leave there for China. I had no money, and when I heard you were going to British Columbia, I wished to go with you."

"It'll be rough."

"It often is." He looked at me, not smiling. "It can be rough in China, too." He paused. "My father was an official in the western desert country, in what we called the New Territories. It is a land where all people ride, as they do here."

A low wind moaned in the grass, and long ripples ran over the far plain. It would be dawn soon. The cattle were beginning to get up, to stretch and to graze.

When I was in the saddle, I looked back at him. "Can you use a rifle?"

"Our compound was attacked several times by bandits," he said. "We all had to shoot."

"Before this is over, you may have another chance," I said.

9

Chapter II

We were four hours into the morning when Cap Rountree stood in his stirrups, shading his eyes as he looked off to the north. Then he waved us west and came cantering back to meet me as I rode up from riding drag.

"There's been a prairie fire. There's no more grass."

"How about going east? We have to ride east, anyway, to hook up with Orrin."

"The fire came from the east. The way I figure, the grass back thataway is burned off. Westward we've got a chance because of that mite of rain we had night before last. That could have put out the fire."

That made sense. "Stay with the herd," I said, "and I'll scout off to the west."

"Keep your Winchester handy. I cut some Injun sign over yonder."

Sure enough, I'd not gone a quarter of a mile before I rode up to the edge of the burn. Far as the eye could see, the prairie was black. Turning west, I cantered along for a ways, studying the country. The raindrops had speckled the burned grass, and the chances were Cap's guess was right. Nobody knew more about handling cattle in rough country than Cap.

Several times, I came upon buffalo tracks, and they had turned off to the west just as we were doing. This was going to set us back a day or two, and it was time we could ill afford to lose. It was just spring, with the grass turning green, but we had a long drive ahead and must reach our destination before winter set in.

Every time I topped a rise, I studied the country around, but mostly what lay behind. There were always a few antelope in sight and usually buffalo, but in small bunches and afar off.

Just short of midday, we swung the herd into a shallow valley where there was a slough and some good grass. Lin went off to one side and put together a small fire.

Nobody takes a herd over two thousand miles of rough country without trouble. We'd have our share, and we were ready for it, but we didn't want more than we had to have.

Tyrel came in from the herd, and getting down from the bay he was riding, he whipped the dust from him with his hat, standing well back. When he came up to the fire for coffee, he looked over at me. "See anything?"

He'd seen me looking around when I topped those rises. "Nothing but buffalo," I said.

"I got a bad feeling," he said.

"You and me both," I said.

Cap rode in and dismounted, switching his saddle to a rat-tailed dun that looked like the wrath of God but was tougher than whalebone, a mustang born to the wide plains and the rough country.

When he came up to the fire, he glanced from one to the other. "If you want to know what I think—"

"I do," I said.

"We better skip that drive east. Allowin' there's good grass like we heard, we still lose time, and we just ain't got it to lose."

He filled his cup and came over, squatting on his heels. He took a stick and drew in the dust. "Right here's about where we are. Right over here is the Jim River—the James if you want to be persnickety about it. I say we drive west, then follow the Jim north, which gives us water all the way.

"Right here there's a mighty pretty valley where the Pipestem flows into the Jim. We can let the cattle have

11

a day there, which will give Orrin a chance to gain on us.

"There's good grass in that valley, and there's a lot of elm, box elder, and some cottonwood along the rivers. There'll be firewood and shade for the stock if we have to wait, and it might pay to wait a couple of days for Orrin."

"We've been lucky on the grass," Tyrel said, "bein' so early in the year, but we're drivin' north."

"You're durned right." Cap sipped his coffee. "An' from here on, the new grass will be slower, and farther west it will be almighty scarce."

Well, now. That fitted in with my own thinking, but I studied on it a mite. Orrin was probably on the river right now, ridin' one of them steamboats up the Red River to Pembina. Once he got there, he'd have to find a couple of men, buy teams and a couple of Red River carts, then stock up with supplies for the westward drive.

He would need a day if he was lucky, three days if he wasn't, and then he would start west to meet us. We would be coming up from the south, and he would be driving west.

From Pembina there was a trail that led due west through the Pembina Mountains and skirting the Turtle Mountains on the north. If Orrin could make his arrangements in Pembina, he could strike west along that trail, and with luck we'd meet him somewhere close to the Mouse River. With horse-drawn carts, he should make about twenty miles a day, while we would make no more than twelve to fifteen. If he had to go on to Fort Garry, that would throw everything out of kilter, and we'd have to meet farther north.

We scratched around in the dirt, indicating trails and figuring how best to go. Here and there, we'd picked up word of what to expect. We'd stay with the Jim as far as we could, then strike west-northwest for the Canadian border.

"Wish we had more men," Cap said. "The Sioux can be mighty ornery."

"We'll have to chance it." I went out to the remuda and threw my saddle on a rangy buckskin.

It was a worrisome thing. The last thing I'd wanted was a cattle drive through country I'd never seen. Aside from Cap and Tyrel, the other men were strangers, picked up where we could get them. They seemed to be mighty good hands, but only time would show what they were made of, and any time you ride through Sioux and Blackfoot country, you're borrowing trouble.

We were short on grub, long on ammunition, and needful of a tie-up with Orrin. Worst of all, he'd be coming west with strangers, too, if he could recruit any help at all.

It was early spring, with patches of snow still holding on the shady side of the hills. The grass was growing, but mostly it was just like a green mist over the hills, although a lot of last year's grass, cured on the stem, was still out there.

Logan had said we could expect Higginses, and the name of Higgins, some folks with whom we'd had a long-running feud, was our name for trouble. Some of those Higgins boys could really shoot.

After I'd had a bite, I swung into the saddle and rode out to relieve one of the boys watching the cattle. He was a new boy we'd found riding south for Abilene, and he stopped at our fire. When we heard he was hunting a riding job, we told him he had one if he was a stayer.

"Never quit nothin' yet," he said, "until it was done."

"You got a name you want to use?"

"Isom Brand. Folks call me Brandy."

"All right. Now think on this. You hook up with us, you'll be riding into wild country, Injun country. You'll see mountains like you've never seen and wider plains than you can believe. You're likely to miss a meal or two, as we're short of grub until we hook up with my brother Orrin, but we don't want anybody who is likely to complain."

He just looked at me, that smooth-faced kid with the quick blue eyes, and he said, "You goin' to miss those meals, too?"

"We miss them together," I said.

"You hired a hand," he said. He hesitated then, flushing a little. "I ain't got much of an outfit. I give all I had left in cash money to my ma for her and sis afore I pulled out."

"Couldn't you find a job close to home?"

"No, sir. There just weren't none."

"They got enough money to last?"

"No, sir. I have to send some to them as soon as I can."

"You shape up," I said, "and I'll advance you some."

He was riding a crow-bait plow horse that was no good for our work, so we turned him into the remuda, and we roped a paint we bought off an Injun. Brandy topped him off all right, and we rode along.

He was walking a circle on the far side of the herd when I came up to him. "Better go in and get yourself a bite," I suggested, "and catch yourself some shuteye. We won't be moving out for about an hour."

There was water a-plenty and good grass, so we took some time. Meanwhile, keeping a watch out and seeing none of the cattle got to straying, I thought about Logan.

Logan and his twin brother Nolan were Clinch Mountain Sacketts, almost a different breed than us. They were rough boys, those Clinch Mountain Sacketts, right down from ol' Yance Sackett, who founded the line way back in the 1600s. He settled so far back in the mountains that the country was getting settled up before they even knew he was there.

Some of those Clinch Mountain Sacketts were Blockaders; least that's what they were called. They raised a lot of corn up in the mountains, and the best way they could get it to market was in liquid form. They began selling by the gallon rather than the bushel.

Pa, he would have none of that. "If'n you boys want

to take a drink, that's your business, but buy it in town, don't make it. Maybe I don't agree with the government on all things, but we elected them, a majority of us did, and it's up to us to stand by them and their laws.

"From all I hear handed down," he added, "that Yance was a wild one, and his get are the same. Those boys are rougher than a cob, but if you're in trouble, they'll come a runnin'. They'll build you a fire, lend you money, feed you, give you a drink from the jug, or he'p you fight your battles. Especially he'p you fight battles. Why, ain't one of them Clinch Mountain Sacketts wouldn't climb a tree to fight a bear.

"Why, there was a man over at Tellico whupped one of them boys one time. Sure enough, come Saturday night, here was that Sackett again, and the feller whupped him again. An' ever' Saturday night, there was Sackett awaitin' on him, an' ever' time he whupped that Sackett, it got tougher to do. Finally, that feller just give up and stayed to home. He was afraid to show his face because Sackett would be waitin' on him.

"Finally that feller from Tellico, he just taken out and left the country. Went down to the settlements and got hisself a job. He was a right big man, make two of Sackett, but it was years before he stopped jumpin' if you came up behind and spoke to him. 'Made a mistake,' he said after. 'I should have let him whup me. Then I'd of had some peace. Wust thing a man can do is whup a Sackett. They'll dog you to your dyin' day.'"

That was the way it was. If one of us was in difficulties, Logan would come a-runnin', and the least we could do was go see what we could do.

He said he needed beef cattle, so we'd take him beef cattle. I don't know what had him treed up yonder, but it must've been somethin' fierce, knowin' Logan.

So we'd spent all we had, barrin' a few dollars in pocket, and we were headed into wild, rough country with eleven hundred head of steers. But it wasn't only that Logan was in trouble. It was because a Sackett had given his word.

I hear tell that down in the towns some folks don't put much store in a man's word, but with us it was the beginning and the end. There were some poor folks up where we come from, but they weren't poor in the things that make a man.

Through the long afternoon, we plodded steadily west, the blackened earth only a few hundred yards off on our right. The low gray clouds broke, and the sky cleared. The grass was changing, too. We rarely saw the tall bluestem that had grown further east. Now it appeared only in a few bottoms. There was a little bluestem, June grass and needle grass.

Slowly, the herd was gettin' trail broke. Once in a while, some old mossyhorn steer would make a break to go home, and we'd have to cut him back into the herd, but generally they were holdin' steady. A rangy old brindle steer had taken the lead and held it. He was mean as a badger with his tail in a trap and would fight anything that argued with him, so mostly nobody did.

Cap rode back to me just about sundown as we were rounding the stock into a hollow near a slough. "Tell," he said, "better come an' have a look whilst it's light."

He led the way to the far side of the slough, and we studied the ground. The grass was pressed down here and there, the remains of a fire and the tracks of two travois.

"Six or seven, I'd say," Cap said, "but you're better at this than me."

Well, I took a look around. "Six or seven," I agreed. "Maybe eight. One of them travois leaves a deep trail, and I figure they've got a wounded man on it.

"They've had them a fight," I said, "and that's odd because there's at least two women along. It's no war party."

"There's a papoose, too," Cap said. "If you look yonder by that rock, you'll see where they leaned his cradle board."

I indicated a dirty piece of cloth lying in the trampled-down grass. It was very bloody. "Somebody is hurt," I said. "Probably the man on the travois."

Squatting, I sat on my heels and looked over the place where they'd camped and the ashes left from their fire. "Yesterday," I said, "maybe the day before."

"And they're headin' west, like us."

"We got to keep an eye out. We'll be comin' up with them maybe tomorrow night or next morning. They aren't going to make much time."

"What do you make of it?" Cap asked.

"A papoose in the cradle board, one walkin' about youngster, two women and four men. Two of the men are oldish, gettin' on in years. One's a youngster—fightin' age but young. Then there's the wounded man."

"I spotted 'em a while back." Cap put the butt of his rifle on the ground. "They've been keepin' to low ground. Looks to me like they're scared."

Well, I took my hat off and wiped the sweat off my forehead, then put my hat on and tugged her down tight. "Cap," I said, "we'd best sleep light and step careful because whatever's after them is comin' our way, too."

Chapter III

We were taking it easy. We had a long way to go, but the season was early, and there was no use us gettin' so far north that the grass wouldn't have come yet. The country was greenin', but it would take time. We had come up to the Jim River just below Bear Creek.

Cap an' Tyrel scouted ahead, riding into the trees to see if company waited on us, but there was nobody. There was fair grass on the plain and mighty good grass in the creek bottom, so we swung our herd around and bedded them down.

Swingin' along the edge of the trees, I dabbed a loop on a snag and hauled it up for the fire. Lin was already down from the wagon and picking up some flat stones he could use to set pots on.

We hadn't any chuck wagon, and grub was scarce. Leavin' Brandy with the stock, Tyrel rode down to where I sat my horse. "Saw some deer back yonder." He gestured toward the creek. "Figured I'd ride out and round up some meat."

"Sure." As he turned his mount away, I said, "Keep your eyes open for those Injuns. I think they're somewhere about."

"Maybe so." He pulled up for a moment. "Night before last—maybe I was wrong, but I thought I smelled smoke." He let it rest for a minute, and then he said, "Tell? You know what I think? I think those Injuns are ridin' in our shadow. For protection, like."

He took out his Winchester and rode off into the trees, but what he said stayed with me. Those Indians were only a handful, and they'd seen trouble from

18

somebody. Tyrel might be right, and they could be stayin' close to us with the idea that they'd not be attacked with us so close by.

By the time I started back for camp, the cattle had settled down. A few were still grazing on last year's grass, but most of them were full as ticks. I wasn't fooled by their good shape because I knew rough country lay ahead of us.

When I stepped down from the saddle and ground hitched my horse, the other two riders had come in and were drinkin' coffee. Gilcrist was a lean, dark man who handled a rope well and seemed to know something about stock but was obviously a gambler. He'd not had much luck getting up a game around camp because mostly when we bedded down the cattle, we were too tired to do anything but crawl into our blankets ourselves. The man traveling with him was a big, very heavy man but not fat. He was no taller than me, maybe even a mite shorter, but he was a good fifty pounds heavier, and it wasn't fat. Gilcrist called him the Ox, so we followed suit. Nobody ever did ask him his name, as folks just didn't ask questions. Whatever somebody named you or whatever you answered to was good enough.

Just as I was stepping down from my bronc, I heard a rifle shot. "We'll have fresh meat for supper," I said.

Gilcrist glanced around. "Suppose he missed?"

"That was Tyrel. He doesn't miss."

A few minutes later, Tyrel rode into camp with the best parts of a deer. He unloaded the meat at the fire and led his horse away to strip its gear. Nobody said anything, but when Tyrel came back into camp, I noticed Gilcrist sizing him up.

We ate, and Tyrel spoke quietly to me. "They're about, Tell. I spotted one of them watchin' me." He paused a moment. "I left them a cut of the meat."

"He see you?"

"Uh-huh. I laid it out nice and ready for him. I think they're hard up."

I turned to Gilcrist and the Ox. "When you finish, ride out and let Cap and Brandy come in."

The Ox wiped his hands on his pants. "Do the kid good to wait a mite. Teach him something."

I looked across the fire at him. "If he needs teaching, I'll teach him. You relieve him."

The Ox leaned back on his elbow. "Hell, I just got here. They can wait."

"Relieve him," I said, "now."

The Ox hesitated, then slowly got to his feet, deliberately prolonging the movements. "Oh, all right," he said. "I'll go let mama's little boy come in."

He mounted his horse and rode out. Gilcrist got to his feet, then commented, "Better go easy with him. He's a mighty mean man."

"Where I come from they're all mean if you push them," I said. "If he stays on this job, he'll do his work."

Gilcrist looked around. "Mighty big country out here. Looks to me like a man could do what he wanted."

"Boot Hill is full of men who had that idea." Tyrel spoke casually, as if bored. "It's a big country, all right, big enough for men who are big enough."

Gilcrist mounted up and rode out, and Tyrel threw his coffee on the grass. "Looks like trouble."

"I saw it when I hired them, but who else could I get? Nobody wanted to ride north into wild country."

"Maybe they wanted to. Maybe they had reason."

"That big one," I commented, "looks strong enough to wrassle a bull. Maybe I should save him for Logan. Logan likes his kind."

"Maybe. Maybe you won't be able to save him, Tell. Maybe he won't wait that long."

Cold winds blew down from the north, and there were occasional spitting rains. The scattered patches of snow were disappearing, however, and the trees along the river bottoms were green. There were pussywillows along the bottoms, too, and patches of crocus growing near the snow.

We moved north, day after day, following the course of the James River but holding to the hills on one side or the other.

As we came down the hill into the valley where the James and Pipestem met, Tyrel rode over to where I was. "Cold," he said, meanin' the wind, "mighty cold!"

"There's wood along the river," I said, "and we'll rest up for a couple of days. It's needful that Orrin have time. No tellin' whether he'll find the men we need or not."

"Wish we could get rid of them two." Tyrel gestured toward the Ox and Gilcrist. "I just don't cotton to them."

"Nor me," I said, "an' old Cap is keepin' his mouth shut, but it's hard."

Turning to look at him, I said, "Tye, all day I've been thinkin' of the mountains back home. Must be I'm gettin' old or something, but I keep thinkin' of how it was back home with ma sittin' by the fire workin' on her patchwork quilt. Night came early in the winter months, and lookin' out the window a body could see pa's lanterns making patterns on the snow as he walked about. He'd be doin' the last of the chores, but when he came in, he always brought an armful of wood for the wood box."

"I recall," Tyrel said. "We sure spent some time climbin' around those mountains! All the way from Chunky Gal to Roan Mountain. I mind the time Orrin got lost over to Huggins Hell and was plumb out of sight for three days."

"I wasn't there then. I'd already slipped along the mountains and over the Ohio to join up with the Union."

"Nolan went t'other way. He rode down to Richmond and joined the Confederacy. We had people on both sides."

"It was that kind of a war," I commented, and changed the subject. "When we were talkin' about who'd been to the north, I clean forgot the drive I made right after the war. Went up the Bozeman Trail into Montana. I didn't stay no longer than to get myself turned around and headed back, although it was a different trail I rode on the return.

"It was on the way up I got my first taste of the Sioux. They're a rough lot, Tyrel. Don't you take them light."

Tyrel chuckled suddenly. "Tell? You mindful of an old friend of yours? The one we called Highpockets?"

"You mean Haney? Sure. Odd you should speak of him. Last time I heard tell of him, he was headed north."

"Mind the time he went to the sing over at Wilson's Cove? He fell head over heels for some visitin' gal from down in the Sequatchie and went at it, knuckle and skull, with some big mule skinner.

"I remember he come back, and he got out what he used to call his 'reevolver', and he said, 'That ol' boy's give me trouble, so I'm a gonna take my ol' reevolver an' shoot some meat off his bones.' He done it, too."

We rounded up our steers in the almost flat bottom of that valley and let them graze on the stand of last year's grass. There was green showin' all about, but mostly what they could get at was cured on the stem. There was water a-plenty, and this seemed like a good time to rest up a mite.

Cap killed a buffalo, a three-year old cow, on the slope above the river, so we had fresh meat. The boys bunched the cattle for night, and Cap said, "We'd best start lookin' for windy hills for campin'. The way I hear it, up north where there's all those rivers, lakes, and such, there's mosquitoes like you wouldn't believe. Eat a man alive, or a horse."

"Mosquitoes?" I said. "Hell, I've seen mosquitoes. Down on the Sulphur—"

"Not like the ones they have up north," Cap said. "You mind what I say, Tell. When you hear stories of them, you'll swear they're lies. Well, they ain't. You leave a horse tied out all night and chances are he'll be dead by morning."

Me, I looked over at him, but he wasn't smiling. Whether he knew what he was talkin' about, I didn't know, but he wasn't funnin'. He was downright serious.

There were mosquitoes there on the Pipestem, but we built a smudge, and it helped some. Nobody talked much, but we lazed about the fire, takin' our turn at watching over the cattle. The remuda we kept in close to camp where we could all more or less keep an eye on it. What Indians wanted most of all was horses, and without them we'd be helpless.

A time or two, I walked out under the stars, away from the campfire and what talk there was, just to listen.

There was no sound but the cattle stirring a mite here and there, rising or lying down, chewing their cuds, occasionally standing up to graze a bit. It was still early.

Later, when I was a-horseback on the far side of the herd, I thought I caught a whiff of wood smoke that came from a different direction than our fire. Well, if they were riding in our shadow, they were no bother, and it was all right with us.

Gave a body a kind of restful feeling, just knowing he wasn't alone out there.

This was a lovely valley, already turning green with springtime, but it was a valley in a great wide open country where we rode alone, where we had no friends, and if trouble came, we'd have to handle it all by our lonesome. There wasn't going to be anybody coming to help.

Not anybody at all.

Chapter IV

For two days, we rested where the Pipestem met the James, holding the cattle on the grass at the edge of the woods and gathering fallen limbs and dead brush for firewood.

"Pleasant place," Tyrel said. "I hate to leave."

Gilcrist glanced over at me. "We pulling out?"

"Just before daybreak. Get a good night's sleep."

Gilcrist finished his coffee and got up. "Come on, Ox, let's relieve mama's boy and the old man."

Tyrel glanced at me, and I shrugged. Lin straightened up from the fire, fork in hand. The Ox caught his expression. "Something you don't like, yellow boy?"

Lin merely glanced at him and returned to his work.

The Ox hesitated, glancing over at me where I sat with my coffee cup in my hands; then he went to his horse, mounted, and followed Gilcrist.

"If we weren't short-handed," I said to Tyrel, "he'd get his walkin' papers right now."

"Sooner or later," Tyrel agreed. Then he added, "The other one fancies himself with a gun."

By first light, we were headed down the trail, climbing out of the valley and heading north. A few miles later, I began angling off to the northwest, and by sundown we had come up with the Pipestem again.

The herd was trail broke now, and the country was level to low, rolling hills. We saw no Indians or any tracks but those of buffalo or antelope. The following day, we put sixteen miles behind us.

Each night, just shy of sundown, Tyrel, Cap, or I would scout the country around. Several times, we

24

caught whiffs of smoke from another campfire, but we made no effort to seek them out.

Short of sundown on the third day, after our rest, I killed a buffalo, and the Ox came up to lend a hand. I never did see a buffalo skinned out faster or meat cut and trimmed any better. I said as much.

"Pa was a butcher, and I growed up with a knife in hand. Then I hunted buffalo on the southern plains."

"Take only the best cuts," I said, "an' leave the rest."

He was bent over, knife in hand. He turned his head to look at me. "Leave it? For varmints?"

"There's some Indians close by, and they're having a bad time of it. Leave some for them."

"Injuns? Hell, let 'em rustle their own meat. What d'we care about Injuns?"

"They're hungry," I said, "and their best hunter is wounded and laid up."

Obviously, he believed me crazy. "I never knew an' Injun worth the powder it took to kill him."

"Back in the mountains," I said, "I knew quite a few. Generally speakin', they were good folks.

"We had trouble with them a time or two and they're good, tough fightin' men. I've also hunted and trapped with them, slept in their lodges. They are like everybody else. There's good an' bad amongst them."

We left some meat on the buffalo hide, and I stuck a branch in the ground and tied a wisp of grass to it. Not that they'd need help findin' it.

Come daylight, when we moved out with the cattle, I took a look, and every last bit of meat was gone, and the hide, also. I counted the tracks of a boy and two women. They'd have read the sign and would know that meat was left a-purpose.

With Cap ridin' point, the cattle strung out along the trail, and I rode drag. Tyrel was off scoutin' the country. Pipestem Creek was east of us now, and the country was getting a mite rougher. Maybe it was my imagination. Off on the horizon, far ahead and a hair to the west, I could see the top of a butte or hill.

By noontime, that butte was showing strong and clear. It was several hundred feet high and covered with timber. When Tyrel came back to the drag, I rode ahead to talk to Cap.

"Heard of that place," he said. "They call it the Hawk's Nest. There's a spring up yonder—good water."

After a bit, he added, "Big lake off to the north. Maybe a mite east. Devil's Lake, they call it. Got its name, they say, from a party of Sioux who were returning victorious from a battle with the Chippewa. Owanda, the Sioux medicine man, had warned them not to make the attack, but they were young bucks, eager for battle and reputation, and they didn't listen.

"Their folks were watching from the shore, saw them coming far out on the lake, and could tell from the scalps on the lifted lances that they'd been victorious.

"Well, some say that night came down. It had been dusk when they were sighted. Night came, but the war party didn't. That day to this, nobody's seen hide nor hair of them. Devils in the lake, the Injuns say."

"Owanda must have been really big medicine after that," I commented.

"You can bet he was. But the way I hear it, he was one of the most powerful of all medicine men. Lot of stories about him. First I heard of him was from the Cheyenne."

Cap went on to his flank position, and I took over the point, riding well out in front, studying the country as we moved. Wherever possible, I held the herd down off the skyline. We didn't want to get in the bottoms and among the trees but at least as low as we could move while handling the cattle. There were Indians about, and if they did not know of us now, they would very soon, but I wanted to attract as little attention as possible.

At the same time, I was studying our future. The grass was growing, and soon it would be high enough for grazing. Until then, the cattle would be eating last year's grass. We were getting a jump on the season, and that was why we were not pushing along. We had to stall until the grass was up.

By that time, we should have met with Orrin and his Red River carts. Or so we hoped.

Westward the drive was long. The camp for which we were headed was in rugged mountain country, and we had to make it before the snow started falling. Once the grass was up and we had Orrin with us, we'd have to push hard, even at the risk of losing flesh from those steers.

Tyrel and me, we didn't even have to talk to know what the other one was thinking. It was almost that way with Cap.

Gilcrist and the Ox were worrisome men. Tyrel was right when he said Gilcrist fancied himself with a gun, and while I'd never wanted the reputation of gunfighter, a reputation both Tyrel and me had, I kind of wished now Gilcrist knew something about us. Might save trouble.

Many a man thinks large of himself because he doesn't know the company he's in. No matter how good a man can get at anything, there's always a time when somebody comes along who's better.

It was Tyrel who worried me, too. Tyrel was a first-class cattleman, a good man with handling men, and he never hunted trouble, but neither did trouble have to look very far to find him. Orrin an' me, we might back off a little and give a trouble-huntin' man some breathin' space.

Not Tyrel—you hunted trouble with him, you'd bought yourself a packet. He didn't give breathing space; he moved right in on you. A man who called his hand had better be reaching for his six-shooter when he did it.

Worst of it was, he seemed kind of quiet and boy-like, and a body could make a serious mistake with him.

Back in the high-up hills where we came from,

fightin' was what we did for fun. You got into one of those shindigs with a mountain boy and it was root hog or die. Pa, who had learned his fightin' from boyhood and seasoned himself around trappers' rendezvous, taught us enough to get started. The rest we picked up ourselves.

The wind was picking up a mite, and there was a coolness on it that felt like rain, or snow. It was late in the season for snow, but I'd heard of snow in this country when it was summer anywhere else. When we were close to the Hawk's Nest, we bedded them down for the night.

"Lin, feed 'em as quick as ever you can," I said to the cook. "I think we're sittin' in for a spell of weather." I pointed toward the Hawk's Nest. "I'm going up yonder to have a look over the country before it gets dark."

The Hawk's Nest was a tree-capped butte rising some four hundred feet above the surrounding country, and when I topped out, I found a gap in the trees and had a good view of the country.

There was a smoke rising about a mile up the creek from where we were camped at the junction of the Pipestem and the Little Pipestem. Far ahead, I could see a line of green that showed the Pipestem curved around to the west. Somewhere off there was the Sheyenne.

The water in the spring was fresh and cold. I drank, then watered the line-back dun I was riding and swung into the saddle. Just as I was starting to come off the top, I glimpsed another smoke, only this one was to the west of us and seemed to be coming from a bottom along the Pipestems as it came from the west and before it began its curve toward the south.

It lay somewhat to the west of the route we should be taking on the morrow but not so far off that it wasn't cause for worry.

For a time, I just sat there under cover of the last trees and studied that layout. I brushed a big horsefly off the shoulder of the dun and said, "You know,

Dunny, this here country is sure crowdin' up. Why, there's three smokes goin' up within a five-mile square. Gettin' so it ain't fittin' for man or beast."

Then I turned that dun down trail and headed for the beef and beans. Seemed so long since I'd eaten, my stomach was beginnin' to think my throat was cut.

By the time I reached the fire, Cap an' Brandy were just finishing up. Cap glanced over at me, and I said, "We've got neighbors."

"I seen some tracks," Cap said.

"How many?"

"Four, looked like. Shod horses. Big horses, like you find up here in the north where you have to buck snow in the wintertime."

"There's no way we're going to hide eleven hundred head of cattle," I said, "but we won't start westerin' for a bit. Come daybreak, we'll hold on the North Star."

"Back in Texas," Cap said, "when night came, we used to line up a wagon tongue on the North Star. Use it for a pointer."

Lin handed me a tin plate full of beans and beef, and I took a look at Brandy. He was settin' quiet, almighty serious for a boy his years.

"You havin' any trouble?" I asked him.

He gave me a quick look. "No, not really."

"Stand clear if you can," I said. "That's a mean lot."

"I can take care of myself."

"I don't doubt it. But right now I need every man, need 'em bad. Once we hook up with Orrin, it may be some better, but we don't know. Understand, I'm not puttin' any stake rope on you. A man just has to go his own way."

Brandy went out to throw his saddle on a fresh horse, and Cap looked up from his coffee. "He's makin' a fair hand, Tell, and he's got the makin's."

Well, I knew that. Trouble was I had to walk almighty careful not to step on his pride. No matter how rough it was, a man has to saddle his own broncs in this western country. Only I was afraid Brandy was goin' to have to tackle the big one before he'd whupped anybody his own size. It didn't seem fair, but then, a lot of things aren't. We take them as they come.

If I was around—

But who knew if I would be?

The Ox looked fat, but he wasn't. He was just heavy with bone and muscle, and his broad, hard-boned face looked like it had been carved from oak. He was a man of tremendous strength, with thick arms, massive forearms, and powerful hands. He gave me the feeling of a man who has never seen anything he couldn't lift or any man who could even test him.

I said as much to Tyrel. "Gilcrist told me he'd seen him break a man's back just wrasslin' for fun."

"I don't think he ever did anything just for fun," I said.

Tyrel nodded. "You be careful, Tell. That Ox ain't human. He's a brute."

"I want no part of him," I replied.

On most cow outfits, a man stands night guard about two hours at a time, but we were short-handed and in wild country. The Ox and Gilcrist were going to be on from six to ten, Cap and Brandy would take over from ten until two, with Tyrel and me closing out until morning when one of us would come in, get the fire started, and awaken Lin so's he could fix breakfast.

If we were going to be attacked by Indians, it would most likely occur just before daybreak, but nobody has any certainty of any such thing.

When Cap touched me on the shoulder, it was just shy of two, and I was up, tugging on my boots. Under a tree about thirty yards away, Tyrel was already on his feet. We made it a rule to sleep apart, so if somebody closed in on one of us, the other could outflank them. There were those who thought we'd be better off side by side, but we figured otherwise. Too easy for one man to hold a gun on us both.

All was quiet, the cattle resting. The stars were

bright, here and there blotted by clouds. A body could see the darkness of the trees, the lumped bodies of the cattle, and hear the footfalls of a horse as it moved.

It was past three, closing in on four o'clock before it started to grow gray. The line-back dun was moving like a ghost toward a meeting with Tyrel. Suddenly, the dun's head came up, ears pricked. My Winchester slid into my hands, and at that moment I saw Tyrel.

He was sitting quiet in the saddle, his hands on his thighs, reins in the left hand.

Facing him were four Sioux warriors.

Chapter V

Now I'd lay a hundred to one those Injuns had never seen a fast draw, but if one of them lifted a weapon, it would be the last thing they ever did see.

At that range, there was just no way he was going to miss, and that meant he would take out two for sure, and likely he'd get three. Time and again, I've seen him fire, and men would swear he'd fired once when actually he'd fired twice and both bullets in a spot the size of a two-bit piece.

They'd never seen a fast draw, but they were fighting men, and there was something about him, just a-settin' there quiet with his hand on his thigh that warned them they'd treed a bad one.

Their eyes were riveted on him, so I was within fifty feet and moving in before they saw me, and I was on their flank.

"Something wrong, Tyrel?" I asked.

He never turned his head, but he spoke easy. "Looks like I was about to find out."

One big Indian turned his pony to face me, and the minute he did, I recognized him. "Ho! I see my old friend, High-Backed Bull!" I said.

He looked to be as tall as my six feet and four inches, and he was heavier, but a lean, powerful man. He was darker than most, with high cheekbones and a Roman nose. He stared at me.

"I have no friend who is white eyes," he said.

Me, I pushed my hat brim back so's he could see my face a little better. "You and me, Bull, we had a nice run together. That was years back, down on the Bozeman Trail.

"You were a mighty strong man," I added, "a big warrior." I doubled my biceps and clapped a hand to it, then pointed at his. "Much strong!" I said. "Run very fast."

He peered at me. *"Sack-ETT!"* he shouted. *"You Sack-ETT!"*

I grinned at him. "Long time back, Bull!" Now I knew he had no liking for me. He'd tried to kill me then, not from any hatred of me but simply because I was a white man driving cattle over the Bozeman Trail, which the Sioux had closed to us. They'd caught me, stripped me, and had me set to run the gauntlet, only I'd started before they were ready and had broken free, taking off across the country. John Coulter had done it one time, and maybe there was a chance.

They came after me, the whole lot of them, only I'd been running in the mountains since I was a youngster, and I began putting distance between us. All but this one, the one they called High-Backed Bull. Soon it was just the two of us, him and me, and a good mile off from the rest, and he throwed a spear at me.

It missed by a hair, and then he closed in on me, running fast. Dropping suddenly, he spilled right over me, and he was up, quick as a cat, but I was up, too, and when he come at me, I throwed him with a rolling hip lock as pa had showed me long ago. I throwed him, all right, and throwed him hard. He hit the ground, and I grabbed up his spear and was about to stick him with it.

He'd been stunned by the shock of hitting the ground, just for a moment, like. He stared up at me, and he was such a fine-lookin' man, I just couldn't do it. I just broke the spear across my knee, threw down the pieces, and I taken out across country.

Some of the Injuns had gone back for ponies, and they were coming at me when I made the trees atop a knoll. They come up, a-runnin', and I scrooched down

33

behind a bush, and when this rider paused to swing his pony between two trees, I hit him across the small of the back with a thick branch I'd picked up.

It knocked him forward and off balance, and in a moment I was jerkin' him off the pony and swingin' to its back.

We ran those ponies, me ahead and them after me, until the sun went down, but I'd circled around and came back to where my outfit was camped. I went through patches of woods, across plains, down rocky draws, and finally I seen ol' Tilson's high-top sombrero against the sky, and I called out, "Don't shoot, Til! It's me! Sackett!"

Well, they'd give me up for dead. Two days the Injuns had me, and there'd been a third day of gettin' away from them.

"Where the hell you been? We're short-handed enough," Til said, " 'thout you taken off a Sundayin' around over the hills whilst the rest of us work."

"I was took by Injuns," I said.

"A likely story!" he scoffed. "You've still got your hair."

He pointed toward camp. "Get yourself some coffee. You'll be standin' guard at daybreak."

Well, I walked down into camp, and ol' Nelson was standin' there by the fire. "You bring any company with you?" he asked.

"Tried to avoid it," I said, "but there might be one of them show up. I done some runnin'," I said, "and then I got this horse."

"You call that a *horse*. Won't weigh six hundred pound."

"Don't you miscall him. He can *run*."

Nelson took up a cup and filled it. "Have yourself something." He looked at me. "You et?"

"Oh, sure! Don't you worry none about me! Why, two, three days ago, I et at a cow camp run by Nelson Storey, who was takin' cows to Montana. I ain't had a bit since, but then what can a man expect? I didn't come up on no rest-too-rawnts, and them Injuns didn't figure to waste grub on a man who wasn't goin' to live long enough to digest it."

He pointed. "There's some roast buffalo, camp-baked beans, and some prunes. That should fix you up." He took out a big silver watch. "You got two hours to sleep before you stand guard."

"Nels," I said, "I lost my rifle, and—"

"One of the boys picked it up," he said. "It's in the wagon. Draw you a new knife there. I'll dock you for the time off."

Well, I knew he wouldn't do no such thing, but I was so glad to be back, I didn't care if he did. Only when I was a-settin' my horse out there by the cattle that night, I thought back to the hatred lookin' at me out of those fierce black eyes of High-Backed Bull, and I was glad I'd seen the last of him.

Until now—

He stared at me. "You *Sack-ETT*," he said.

Tyrel said, "You actually *know* this Injun?"

"I know him," I said, "from that trip I took up the Bozeman Trail after the War Between the States. We had us a little run-in back yonder. They had me fixed to run the gauntlet—fifty-sixty big Injuns all lined up with me to run down the aisle betwixt 'em and each one hittin' or cuttin' at me.

"Well, I recalled that story pa told us about John Coulter, so I done likewise. I just taken off across the country and not down their gauntlet. This big buck here, he durned near caught me."

"So Sack-ETT," Bull said, "it is again."

Smiling, I held out my hand. "Friends?" I said.

He stared at me. "No friend," he said. "I kill."

"Don't try it. I'm bad luck for you. Me," I said, "bad medicine for you, much bad medicine."

He stared at me, very cool and not at all scared. "Soon you hair here." He touched his horse's bridle where three other scalps, one of them obviously that of a white man, already dangled.

He changed the subject. With a wide sweep of his hand, he said, "This belong to Sioux. What you do here?"

"Crossing it, Bull. We're just driving across on the way to Fort Qu'Appelle." It was a Canadian fort, and the name just came to me. "Maybe we'll meet on the way back."

They turned and rode away, and Tyrel, he just sat there looking after them, and then he shook his head. "There was a time there when I figured I'd have to do the fastest shootin' I ever done."

Gilcrist and the Ox come ridin' up. They could see the four Sioux ridin' away. "What happened?" Gil asked.

"No trouble," I said. "Just a Sioux who tried to take my hair one time, thinkin' about another try."

"You *knew* him?"

"Some years back," I said. "I'd just come out of the Sixth Cavalry and—"

"The *Sixth?*" He was surprised. "Sackett? Were you *that* Sackett?"

"So far as I know, I was the only one in the outfit."

"I'll be damned," he said. "I'll be dee-double damned!"

"That was a long time ago," I said. "Let's get 'em movin'!"

We lined them out and pointed them north and prayed a little that we wouldn't meet any more Sioux, but after my meeting with High-Backed Bull, I knew they'd be back.

Cap rode up to see me at point. "Hustle 'em, Cap. I want distance."

"You know you ain't goin' to outrun any Injuns," he said. "If they come for us, they'll find us."

"They'll come," I said.

"You should've killed him when you had the chance."

Brandy had come up to us, wanting to hear. "I'd

figure him grateful," Brandy said. "You let him live when you could've killed him."

"They don't figure that way, son," Cap remarked. "They figured him a coward for not followin' through. They don't think he had nerve enough.

"Injuns don't think the same as us, and we keep thinkin' they do. That's been the cause of most of the trouble. We think one way, they think another, and even when the words are the same, they mean different things.

"I've fought 'em here and there, lived with some of them, too. They're good people, mostly, but there's right-out bad ones, the same as with us.

"Folks get the wrong idea about Injuns. Somebody figured the Injuns thought the white man was somethin' special. Some easterner who'd never seen an Injun figured it that way. Nothing of the kind. The Injuns mostly looked down on the white man.

"Why? Because he was tradin' for furs, and the Injuns figured if he was any kind of a man, he'd go ketch his own. He traded for 'em because he didn't know how to hunt or trap.

"The Sioux, the Cheyenne, an' all them, they despised the white man, although they wanted what he traded. They wanted steel traps, guns, blankets, and whiskey."

Cap pushed a brindle steer back into the herd. "Some folks figured it was all wrong to trade the Injuns whiskey, and no doubt it was, but it wasn't meanness made 'em do it. They traded the Injuns whiskey because it was what most of those white men wanted themselves, so they figured the Injun wanted it, too."

We pushed 'em on into the evening and bedded down on Rocky Run, finding ourselves a little hollow down off the skyline. The mosquitoes were worse, but we were a whole lot less visible.

When we had a fire going, I roped a fresh horse and switched saddles. "I'll mosey around a mite," I told

Cap. "You an' Tyrel, you keep a hold on things whilst I'm gone."

"We'll try," Cap said.

Rocky Run was a mite of a stream that probably fed into the James, but there'd been rains, and there was good water. Topping out on a ridge, I dropped over the edge far enough not to skyline myself and took a look around.

Mostly, I studied the country to the west. Come daybreak, we'd be lined out to the west, shaping a bit north for the James again.

How many Sioux were there and how far away?

There'd be a-plenty, no doubt, but I was hoping High-Backed Bull would have to go some distance to his village. There was no way to hide eleven hundred head of cattle and no way you could move them very fast. We'd have to do what we could.

Turning back toward camp, a movement caught my eye. Somebody was coming, somebody on a slow-walking horse that stopped now and again, then started on. But he was coming my way.

Shucking my Winchester, I taken my horse down off the low ridge, kind of angling toward that rider.

It was already almost dark, and there were stars here and yonder, but a body could make things out. This rider was all humped over in the saddle like he was hurt. I caught a momentary glint of metal, and I pulled up and waited.

When he was some fifty yards off, I covered him with my Winchester and let him close the distance.

"Pull up there! Who are you?"

He straightened up then. "What? A *white* man? What're you doing out here?"

"Drivin' some cattle," I said. "What about you?"

"I been runnin'," the man said. "Sioux. I'm headed for Fort Stevenson, Army mail."

"Fort Stevenson? Hell, I didn't know there was a fort up this way. Come on into camp."

He was a fine-looking man, Irish, and with the bearing of a soldier. When I said as much, he said,

"Some years back, in England and India." He threw me a quick glance. "Cattle, you say? Where to?"

"The gold mines," I said.

"It's a long drive," he said, "a very long drive. Strike north toward the South Saskatchewan. You can follow it part of the way. It won't be easy—and stay away from Fort Garry."

"What's wrong?"

"There's trouble brewing. When the Bay Company let go of Rupert's Land, which means most of western Canada, there was no government. It wasn't immediately apparent that Canada was going to take over, so a *métis* named Louis Riel has set up a provisional government."

"Métis?"

"It's a name for the French-Indian or sometimes Scotch-Indian buffalo hunters. Anyway, it looks like trouble, so I'd steer clear of Fort Garry."

"And Pembina?"

"The same."

By now, or very soon, Orrin would be there. He would be right where the trouble was, and he would be alone.

Chapter VI

Orrin Sackett boarded the stage at St. Cloud. Two women were already seated, a short, stout woman with a florid complexion and a young, quite pretty girl in an expensive traveling suit. Seating himself in a corner, Orrin watched the others as they got aboard.

There were three. The first was a square-shouldered, strongly built man in a dark, tailored suit with a carefully trimmed beard. He was followed by two men, roughly dressed and armed with pistols under their coats and rifles in their hands. Scarcely were they seated when, with a pistol-like crack of the whip, they were off.

The man with the trimmed beard glanced at him. Orrin knew he presented a good appearance in his planter's hat, his dark gray frock coat, and trousers of a lighter gray, his dark green vest sporting a fine gold watch chain.

"Fort Abercrombie?" The man asked. "Or are you going further?"

"Fort Garry," Orrin replied. "Or possibly only to Pembina."

"My destination, also. From Georgetown to the steamboat you may have to provide your own transportation. The stage often goes no further than Georgetown. Much depends on the condition of the roads and the disposition of the driver. And, I might add, on the mosquitoes."

Orrin lifted an eyebrow. "The *mosquitoes?*"

"If you have not heard of them, be warned. They

40

are unlike any mosquitoes you will have seen. At least in number. Leave an animal tied out all night and by morning it may be dead. I am serious, sir."

"But what do you do?"

"Stay inside after sundown. Build smudges if you're out. Sleep under mosquito netting. They'll still get you, but you can live with them."

The young girl twisted her lips, obviously disturbed. The two men showed no concern, as if the story were familiar to them, but *what was wrong about them?* He did not wish to stare at them, but there was something, some little thing that disturbed him.

It was not that they were armed. He carried his own pistol in its holster and another, a derringer, in his vest pocket. His rifle was in the blanket roll in the boot. The man with the beard was also armed with a small pistol. Very likely, the women were also, although a woman could, in most cases, travel anywhere in the West in complete safety.

It was not that the two were roughly dressed that disturbed him. He had dressed no better, if as well, for the better part of his life, and in the West men wore whatever was available or what they could afford. Over half the greatcoats one saw were army issue, either blue or gray, and a good number of the hats came from the same source. Yet somehow these men seemed different. Their clothing did not seem to belong to them. They were old clothes and should have been comfortable, but neither man wore them with ease.

"You have been to Fort Garry before? And Pembina?"

The man with the trimmed beard nodded. "Several times, although I am not sure what my welcome will be like this time." He glanced at Orrin again. "They aren't very friendly to outsiders right now."

"What's the problem?"

"They've had an influx of outsiders. Some of them from Ontario but many from the States. Some are land grabbers, some are promoters. You see, when the Bay

Company moved out, they left the country, Rupert's Land, they call it, high and dry and without a government."

He paused, peering from the window. The stage was slowing for a bad place in the road. "The *métis*, the French-Indian people who formerly worked for the company, have lived on their land for several generations. Now, suddenly, there's a question of title. The newcomers say the *métis* own nothing at all.

"Louis Riel has returned from Montreal and is reported to be forming a provisional government. I have met the man but once, in passing, and know nothing about him."

"He's a breed," one of the other men spoke suddenly. "He's part Indian."

His manner of speaking made the statement an accusation, and Orrin said mildly, "Could be in his favor. I've dealt with Indians. They know the country, and some of them are wise men."

The man was about to reply, but seeing the way the conversation was going, the man with the trimmed beard thrust out his hand. "I am Kyle Gavin, and a Scotsman, although I've spent a deal of time in both your country and Canada. We may be of service to each other."

"I am Orrin Sackett, of Tennessee. I have been practicing law in New Mexico and Colorado."

At the name, both the other men glanced up sharply, first at him, and then they exchanged a glance.

Darkness was crowding into the thick brush and trees along the trail, leaning in long shadows across the trail itself. Atop a small hill where some wind was felt, the stage pulled up, and the driver descended.

"I'd sit tight if I was you," he warned. "Keep as many mosquitoes out as you can. I'm lightin' the carriage lamps."

He did so, and then they moved on into the darkness. "There will be food at the next stop," Gavin commented. "I'd advise all to eat. The night will be long."

The road was a mere trace through towering trees, then across open prairies dotted with clumps of brush. Trees had been cut down, but the stumps remained, and occasionally a wheel would hit one of the stumps with a bone-jolting shock. There were strips of corduroy road across marshes, made by laying logs crosswise and covering them with brush and mud.

Inside the coach, all was dark. Orrin removed his hat and leaned his head back against the cushion. In that way, he could doze fitfully, jarred into wakefulness by getting a sharp rap on the skull when the stage passed a bad bump.

After a long time of endless bumping, jolting, and crackings of the whip, a bit of light flickered across his vision. He opened his eyes and, lifting the corner of the curtain, peered out. They had come to a settlement, and only a minute or two later the stage pulled up before a low-roofed building of logs.

The door opened and the stage driver said, "Grub on the table! Better eat up!"

Kyle Gavin got down and turned to offer his hand to the ladies, but the two other men pushed by him and stumbled toward the door.

Exasperated, he started to speak, but Orrin spoke first. "Let them go. It isn't worth the trouble." He waited until both women had been helped to the ground, then said, "Please, let me apologize. Western men are usually thoughtful of womenfolk."

"Thank you, young man," the older woman said. "I live west. I know what the men are like. Those two, they're trouble. I seen it when they got on."

Orrin escorted the two women to the one table, and several men promptly got to their feet, plates in hand. "Set here, ma'am," one of them said.

One of the others turned toward a harried man standing over a stove. "Joe? We've a couple of ladies."

"Yes, sir! Ma'am! Be right there."

Orrin glanced around the room. Several wagons were pulled up outside and at least three saddle horses.

He saw no one whom he knew, but that was expected, for this was new country to him. Yet he searched the faces of the men. Some would be going on to Pembina or Fort Garry, and he badly needed at least two good men.

One was a short, stocky man with a thick neck and a bristle of tight blond curly hair atop his head. There was a deep dentlike scar under his cheekbone. He was one of those who had arisen quickly when he saw the women. He stood to one side now, plate in hand.

"How's the food?" Orrin asked.

The short man threw him a quick, measuring glance. "I've et worse. Matter of fact, it ain't bad."

"Cowhand?"

Shorty shrugged. "Whatever it takes to get the coon. I been a cowhand. I been a timber stiff, too, an' I've driven freight here and there."

"At Pembina or maybe Fort Garry, I'll need a couple of men. A couple who can handle cattle, drive a team, and make a fight if that's necessary."

"Where you goin'?"

"West, through the mountains. They call it British Columbia. I'll pay thirty a month, and the grub's good."

Shorty finished his food. "If you're eatin', you better get up there," he advised. "They don't set no second table."

Orrin Sackett moved up to the table and found a place near the girl who was traveling with them. Passing her a platter of beans and rice, he said, "If there is anything I can do, you have only to ask."

"Thank you."

As she did not seem disposed to talk, he said nothing more but finished his eating and went outside. The two men with rifles were standing near the stage in deep conversation with a third man, pants tucked into his boots, a battered hat pulled low so little of his face could be seen.

Kyle Gavin strolled over and stood near. "Those

men," Gavin commented, "something about them worries me."

"It's the clothes," Orrin replied. "The men don't look like they belonged in them."

"You mean a disguise?"

Orrin shrugged. "Maybe, or maybe just trying to fit into the country." Then he added, "They handle the rifles like they were used to them, though."

The stage rolled on, and again Orrin slept fitfully. Where were Tell and Tyrel? The letter received in St. Paul had stated only that their route would be up the valley of the James, and if they reached the Turtle Mountains first, they would proceed westward, leaving some indication behind.

They were going into wild country, a land unknown to them. Even now, they would be somewhere in Dakota, the land of the Sioux, a fierce, conquering people who had moved westward from their homeland along the Wisconsin-Minnesota boarder to conquer all of North and South Dakota, much of Montana, Wyoming, and Nebraska, an area larger than the empire of Charlemagne.

This land through which they traveled was that which divided the waters flowing south toward the Gulf of Mexico from those flowing north toward Hudson's Bay. There were many lakes, for this was the fabled "land of the sky-blue water," and soon they would be descending into the valley of the Red River of the north.

Orrin awakened suddenly, feeling a head on his shoulder. It was the young lady, who had fallen asleep and gradually let her head fall on his convenient shoulder. He held very still, not wishing to disturb her.

The coach was very dark inside, and he could see little but the gleam of light on the rifle barrels and light where the coach lamps let a glow in through a crack in the curtains. All the rest seemed asleep.

He was about to doze once more when he heard a drum of hoofs on the road behind them. Someone, a fast rider, was overtaking the coach. Carefully, he put his fingers on the butt of his six-shooter, listening.

He heard the rider come alongside and lifted the corner of the curtain but could see nothing, as the rider had already passed too far forward. The stage slowed, and he could hear conversation between the rider and the driver but could distinguish no words.

After a moment, he heard the rider go on, listened to the fading sound of hoof beats, but the stage continued at the slower pace.

A long time later, daylight began filtering through the curtains, and suddenly the girl beside him awakened. She sat up with a start, embarrassed.

"Oh! Oh, I am so sorry!" She spoke softly so as not to disturb the others. "I had no idea!"

"Please do not worry about it, ma'am," Orrin said. "My shoulder's never been put to better purpose."

She tucked away a wisp of hair. Her eyes were brown, and her hair, which was thick and lovely, was a kind of reddish-brown. He suddenly decided that was the best shade for hair, quite the most attractive he'd seen.

He straightened his cravat and longed for a shave. The stubble must be showing. He touched his cheek. Yes, it was He touched his carefully trimmed black moustache.

Kyle Gavin was awake and watching him with a glimmer of amusement in his eyes. Orrin flushed.

He thought again of the short, blond man he had seen at the first stage stop. He looked to be a good man, and it might be hard to find men with all this Riel affair muddying up the waters.

Shorty had looked like the kind who would finish anything he started, and that was the kind of man they would need.

Orrin looked over at Gavin. "What about this Riel affair? What's going to happen?"

"Your guess is as good as mine. The Canadians are sending an army out, but that country north of the lakes is very rugged. We've heard some soldiers were lost. Forty of them, according to one story."

"If Riel wanted to make a fight of it," Orrin suggested, "he could defend some of the narrow rivers through which the army must come. Certainly, with all the woodsmen he would have at his command, that would be simple enough."

"That isn't my understanding," Gavin said. "I was under the impression he wished only to establish a temporary government until the Canadians could take over. But no matter what, we're arriving at a bad time. You, especially, if you want to get men or supplies. What supplies Riel doesn't have, the army will need. You'd better move fast."

"You'll find no men in Fort Garry"—one of the other men spoke up suddenly—"nor any supplies, either. They won't welcome strangers."

"Then you're arriving at a bad time," Orrin suggested, smiling, "aren't you?"

The man stared at him. "Maybe it'll be a bad time for you. I've got friends."

Orrin smiled. "Yes," he said gently, "I suppose everyone has one or two."

Chapter VII

By the evening of the second day, the stage rolled up to a stockade near the Ottertail River. Orrin stepped down and stretched, then extended a hand to the young lady and, after her, to the older woman.

"It isn't much of a place," Orrin said, "but let me look around. I will see what can be found."

"Not much," Gavin admitted. "Last time I was here, it was a good deal more comfortable to sleep in the haymow than inside."

"And the mosquitoes?"

"They'll find you either place. They call this place Pomme-de-Terre, but I can think of several other names for it. Tomorrow we should reach Abercrombie."

"Are there accommodations at the fort?"

"No, but there is in McCauleyville. A chap named Nolan has a fairly decent hotel there."

"And the boat?"

"Probably down river from there." Gavin was watching the two men with rifles. They had gone into the fort at once and disappeared behind some buildings. It was obvious they knew where they were going and what they were about.

Inside the fort, the man behind the bar shook his bald head and rubbed the back of his hand across a stubbled chin. "Mister, we sure ain't set up for ladies. Don't often get womenfolks hereabouts." He jerked his head toward an inner room. "Five beds yonder. Men will sleep three to a bed, mostly, and they ain't finicky."

He was honestly worried. "I seen 'em get off the stage, and I seen trouble. I mean, settin' 'em up. Such womenfolks are expectin' more'n we can offer."

"How about the barn? There's fresh hay, isn't there?"

"Hay? Plenty o' that. Say! Come to think of it, there's the tack room—harness room. Cavalry officers used to keep their horse gear in there."

"How about blankets? And mosquito netting?"

He shook his head. "I got 'em, but only for sale, not for use."

They would need blankets and mosquito netting, too.

"How much for six blankets and netting enough for four?"

He scratched his head, then worried at a piece of paper with a pencil. The figure was excessive but not so much as he'd expected. Nor was the tack room as much of a mess as it might have been.

"We had better eat," Orrin warned them, "and get bedded down before dark. The mosquitoes are coming now."

The younger woman suddenly put out her hand. "I am Devnet Molrone, Mr. Sackett. And this is Mary McCann. She is going to Fort Garry."

"And you?"

"I shall be meeting my brother. He will be at Fort Carlton."

Gavin was surprised. "At Fort Carlton? Is your brother with Hudson's Bay Company?"

It appeared, after some conversation, that her last letter from him had been from Fort Carlton, and she assumed he was located there.

Later, he said to Orrin, "Sackett, if you're going west, you'd best try to keep an eye on that girl. I am afraid she's in trouble." He paused. "You see, Carlton's a trading post, but there aren't too many white men there, and I know most of them. A good lot, on the whole, but unless her brother is employed by the company in closing up some of their operations, I can't see how he'd be there for more than a few days."

Later, over supper, Orrin said, "Tell me about your brother."

"Oh, Doug's older than I am, three years older. He always wanted to hunt for gold, and when he heard of the discoveries out west, nothing would hold him. He wrote to us, told us all about it, and it sounded very exciting. Then, when Uncle Joe died, well, there was nothing to keep him in the East, and Doug was the only living relative I had, so I decided to join him."

Orrin glanced at Gavin. "He knows you're coming?"

"Oh, no! He'd never approve! He thinks girls can't do anything! It's a surprise."

Her eyes were wide and excited. Obviously, she was pleased with her daring and thought he would be equally pleased and surprised.

"Ma'am—Miss Molrone," Orrin spoke carefully. "I think you should reconsider. If your brother was hunting gold, he'd be in British Columbia, and that's a long way, hundreds of miles, west of Fort Carlton.

"Fort Carlton isn't a town, exactly, it's a trading post with a stockade around it. There are a few buildings inside, mostly quarters for those who work there."

She was shocked. "But I thought—I—!"

"Fort Garry is only a small town," Kyle Gavin said, "but I'd suggest you stop there until you locate your brother.

"There's no regular mail, you know. Most of the gold camps are isolated, trusting to someone who brings mail in by boat, horseback, or snowshoes, depending on the situation. And only rarely is there a place where a decent young woman can stay. Your brother probably shares a tent or a small cabin with other men."

Her lip trembled. "I didn't know. I wanted to surprise him. I thought—"

"We can make inquiries at Fort Garry," Gavin suggested. "Some of the *métis* may know him. Or they may remember him."

Suddenly, the realization of what she had done came to her. She put her hand to her mouth. "Oh, my!" Pleadingly, she looked at Gavin, then at Orrin. "I wanted to surprise him. I'm all he's got, you know, now that Uncle Joe is dead."

"Does he know that?"

"How could he? I was going to tell him when I met him. You see, Uncle Joe didn't leave anything. He died very suddenly, and I was alone. I wanted to be with Doug, and so—"

"Don't worry about it," Orrin said. "We'll find him for you."

Later, Kyle Gavin exclaimed, "Sackett? Do you have any idea how tough that will be? To find one man among all those who came west? God knows, he might be dead. There've been men lost in riding the rivers, men killed when thrown by horses or in falls from wagons. The worst of it is," Gavin added, "she's uncommonly pretty."

In the morning, Orrin heated water for her in a bucket and took it to her, then went back outside. The morning was cool, and there were no mosquitoes about. The stage was standing nearby, and the driver and a hostler were hooking up the trace chains.

From the driver Gavin learned the two men with rifles were brothers, George and Perry Stamper. They said they were buffalo hunters.

"Then they've much to learn," Gavin said dryly. "The *métis* have very controlled buffalo hunts. They all work together under rigid discipline. They don't care for the single hunter unless he's just hunting meat for himself or his family."

It was nearly noon when the stage rolled into McCauleyville, close to Fort Abercrombie. They stopped at Nolan's, and Orrin retrieved his blanket-roll and haversack from the boot.

He helped the ladies from the stage and escorted them into the hotel. Nolan's place was clean, the floors mopped as carefully as a ship's deck, curtains at the windows.

Nolan glanced at Gavin, suddenly wary, but said nothing.

"A room for the ladies," Sackett suggested, "and one for me, if available. If not, Mr. Gavin and I will make do."

After the women had been shown to their rooms, Orrin asked, "Know anything about a Douglas Molrone? Probably came through here several months back."

Nolan shook his head. "Night after night, the place is full. It isn't often I know the names of any of them. Going west, was he?"

"Gold hunting."

"Aye, like most of them. He'd be lucky to make it unless he was with a strong party. There's bunches of the Santee Sioux who didn't dare go home after the Little Crow massacre, and they're raiding, taking scalps, stealing horses, usually from the Crees or the Blackfeet, but they'd be apt to attack any small party."

There was, as it chanced, a room for him. Alone, Orrin removed his coat and hung it on a peg in the wall; then he checked his six-shooter. The action was smooth, easy. He hung the cartridge belt and holster over the back of a chair close at hand and, stripping to the waist, bathed as well as he could.

His thoughts skipped westward. Tell and Tyrel should be well into the northern part of Dakota by now and would be wondering about him.

Scowling, he considered Devnet Molrone. She was none of his business, yet could he leave her alone in such a place? He suspected she had little money, possibly only enough to get her to Fort Carlton.

There was nothing wrong with Carlton, but so far as he knew, it was a trading post and little else. No doubt some people had settled around, but they would be few. She would be treated like the lady she was, but no matter, a trading post was simply not equipped or planned to cope with unescorted females.

Would she be any better off in a Red River cart on a trip to nowhere? For the truth was they did not know their exact destination. They would be met—by whom? When? Where? And then what?

Drying himself with the rough towel provided, he slipped on a fresh shirt—somewhere along the line he must have some laundry done or do it himself—then he brushed his coat.

She *was* pretty. Damned pretty!

Nolan was behind the desk worrying over some figures. He pushed his hat back and looked up at Orrin. "Damn it! I never was no hand with figures! Only thing I can count is money, when it's laid right out before me!"

He looked up again. "Where'd you say you was headed, Sackett?"

"We're driving cattle to the gold fields. My brothers are already on the way. Somewhere in Dakota, right now."

"In Dakota? They got to be crazy! That's Sioux country, and those Sioux, they're fighters! Despise the white man, got no use for the Winnebagos, the Crees, or the Blackfeet. They'll fight anybody."

"We hope to have no trouble. We'll be trying to avoid them."

"*Avoid* them? Hah! I doubt if a bird could fly over Dakota without them knowin' it.

"That Molrone girl, huntin' her brother. Like lookin' for one pine needle. But don't you worry none! She'll find herself a husband! Women are almighty scarce, and the way I see it there should be at least one in every family!" He looked up at Orrin, smiling. "A man like you, you should latch onto her. Women that pretty are hard to come by. She's a right pert little lady, too! Gumption, that's what she's got! Took a sight of

53

gumption to come all the way out here huntin' her brother."

He glanced at Orrin. "That feller with you. That Gavin feller, you know him long?"

"Met him on the stage."

"Well, I like you, young feller, and you watch yourself, d'you hear? You be careful."

"Why?"

"I'm just a tellin' you. Watch yourself. Things ain't always what they seem."

"What about this man Riel?"

"Don't know him. Knew his pa. A right good man. He spoke up for the *métis* a time or two. Honest in his dealin's, level-headed man. Owned a mill or something. Good man.

"The young man's just back from Montreal. He was studyin' to be a priest, I heard, then changed his mind, or they changed it for him.

"When those outsiders began to come in with their newfangled way of surveyin', his ma sent for him to come home. She seen trouble comin'.

"I ain't sure he's the right man for it. He's a thoughtful young feller. Seems reasonable. Been through here a time or two.

"Now away out west, the way you're a-goin', there's a man named Dumont, Gabriel Dumont. Captain of the buffalo hunts! Those *métis* would follow him through hell! Good man! A great man! Reminds me of that poem, writ by a man named Gray, somethin' in it about 'Cromwells guiltless of their country's blood' or some such thing. Well, I seen a few in my lifetime! Men who had greatness but no chance to show it elsewhere than here! I seen 'em! I seen a passel of them!"

Nolan glanced at him again. "You ever hear of Frog Town? Well, you fight shy of it. Rob you. Cheat you. Knock you in the head or knife you. That's a bad lot. Sometimes the steamer starts from there, dependin' on how high the water is.

"Steamboatin' on the Red ain't like the Mississippi. Mean. Mean an' cantankerous, that's what it is. River's too high some of the time, too low most of the time, and filled with sawyers, driftin' logs, and sandbars. No fit river for man or beast."

"But it flows north?"

"That it does! That it does!" Nolan put a hand on his sleeve. "Here she comes now, that Molrone girl. Say, is she the pretty one! If I was single—!"

Orrin turned toward her, smiling. She looked up at him. "Oh! Mr. Sackett! I am so glad you are here! They say we must go from here by oxcart, and I was wondering if—?"

"You can go with us. We would have it no other way. And we shall leave tomorrow morning, early."

"I'll be ready."

He paused. "The offer includes Mrs. McCann."

"You want her," Nolan whispered, "you'd better act fast, young feller! She's too durned pretty to be about for long!"

There was a pause, and Nolan pulled his hat brim down and started around the counter. "Don't envy you, young feller. Not one bit! You got a long road to travel, an' it can be mean. Oh, there's folks done it! Palliser done it, the Earl of Southesk, he done it, and, of course, folks like David Thompson, Alexander Henry, and their like, but the Sioux weren't around then, an' there wasn't all this trouble with the *métis*—"

"But you said Riel was a reasonable man?"

"I did, an' I still say it. Trouble is, both them and the army will need grub, they will need rifles and ammunition, and you'll have 'em—if you're lucky."

"You made a reference to Gavin?"

"I said nothing. Only"—he paused—"I like a careful man. I always did like a careful man, and you shape up like such. I said nothing else. Nothing a-tall!"

He started for the door, then turned and came back. "You get smart, young feller. You latch on to that girl.

You'll travel a weary mile before you see her kind again. Ain't only she's pretty, she's game. She's got gumption! That's my kinda woman, boy. That there's my kinda woman!"

Chapter VIII

It was cold and dark when he opened his eyes, holding himself still for a long minute, just to listen. There were subdued rustles from the next room where the women were, so they were already astir.

Rising, he bathed lightly and swiftly, then pulled on his pants and boots and began stropping his razor. The vague light in the room was sufficient until he wished to shave; then he lighted the coal-oil lamp. He shaved with care, and as he shaved, he considered the situation.

With luck they would be aboard the *International* before sundown, and if they hoped to miss the mosquitoes, they must be. Once aboard, he must settle down to some serious thinking, as well as the planning of his every move once he reached Fort Garry.

He rinsed his razor, stropped it once more for the final touch-up, thinking as he did so. It was a foolhardy venture at best, something not to be considered had not a Sackett been in trouble.

You can expect Higginses.

To any Sackett the phrase indicated trouble, but from whom? And why?

Folding his razor, he put it away in its case with his brush and soap, then completed dressing. He rolled his blankets, including his spare pistol, then put out the light.

Taking up his rifle, he stepped to the door, opening it a crack. The air was cool, and he inhaled deeply, waiting and listening.

The small lobby was empty and still. There was no

one at the desk. Sitting near the door was a valise that belonged to Kyle Gavin, but the man himself was nowhere about.

As he put his things down near the door, he noticed part of a torn sticker on the valise . . . *toria*. He straightened up, considering that.

Victoria, B.C.? It could be.

So? Gavin could easily have been there. He was a widely traveled man.

Yet when they had talked of British Columbia, he had offered no information on the area, nor had he mentioned visiting there. Why had Nolan warned him against Gavin? Or about him?

He was opening the door to step outside when he heard a click of heels on the board floor and turned. Devnet Molrone looked fresh and lovely, as though she had not traveled a mile.

"The cart is coming," he said. Even as he spoke, it was pulling up at the door. He was surprised, although he should not have been. He had never seen a Red River cart before, although he had heard of them.

Each cart was about six feet long and three wide; the bottom was of one-inch boards; the wheels were seven and a half feet in diameter. The hubs were ten inches across and bored to receive an axle of split oak. The wood used was oak throughout. Each cart was drawn by a single horse and would carry approximately four hundred pounds. No nails were used. Oak pins and rawhide bindings held it all together.

Kyle Gavin followed the cart and gestured to the driver. "Baptiste, who will drive for us. The ladies will ride in the cart. You and I"—Gavin glanced at Orrin —"will ride horseback. You do not mind?"

Orrin Sackett shrugged. "I prefer to ride. I always feel better on a horse."

Orrin threw his gear into the cart, then placed Devnet's valise and a small trunk in the wagon. Mary McCann had only a valise.

The ungreased axle groaned as they moved out,

Kyle Gavin leading off. Orrin slid his rifle into the boot and swung into the saddle.

The sun was not yet up when they moved out, heading north, parallel to the Red River. There was no sign of the Stampers. As the cart was lightly loaded, they moved out at a good pace.

There was no time for conversation but the route was plain before them. At noon, they pulled up under a wide-spreading elm, and Baptiste set about preparing a meal while the horse, after being watered, was picketed on the thick green grass.

Orrin sat down under the elm's shade, removed his hat, and mopped his brow, his rifle across his lap. His eyes looked off toward the west. "What's over there?" he asked.

Baptiste shrugged a shoulder. "Sand, much sand. Once a sea, I t'ink. Maybe so. Great hills of sand."

"Do you know Riel?"

"Aye, I know him. He is good man—great man. He speaks what we t'ink." He gestured. "We, the *métis,* our home is here. We live our lives on this land. All the time we work. We trap t' fur for Hudson's Bay Company. We have our homes, we raise our children, then the Comp'ny goes away.

"It iss here—*poof!* It iss gone! Then come others, strangers who say we have nothing. They will take our homes. Long ago we call upon Louis Riel, the father. He speaks for us. Now we call upon the son."

"I wish him luck," Orrin said.

Baptiste glanced at him slyly. "You do not come for land? Some mans say Yankees come with army. Many mans."

"That's foolish talk," Orrin replied brusquely. "We've problems of our own without interfering in yours. There are always some folks who make such talk for their own purposes, but the American people wouldn't stand for it."

He squinted his eyes toward the river, frowning a little. Had he seen a movement over there? "As for me,

I'm going to buy a couple of carts and go west to help my brothers with a cattle drive."

Orrin leaned his head back against the tree and closed his eyes. It was cool and pleasant in the shade of the old elm. Kyle Gavin lay only a few yards away, his head pillowed on his saddle. Devnet, also in the shade, was fanning herself with her hat. He liked the way the sun brought out the tinge of red in her hair.

He liked women, and that might be his trouble. A good judge of men, he had proved a poor judge of women in his first attempt, a very poor judge. Yet what was he doing here, anyway? He should be back at home, building friendships before the next election.

He had been a sheriff, a state legislator, and they said he was a man with a future. Yet when a Sackett was in trouble, they all came to help. Old Barnabas, the father of the clan in America, had started that over two hundred years ago. It was a long, long time.

He awakened suddenly, conscious that he had actually slept. Baptiste was harnessing the horse again. Gavin was saddling his horse. Somewhat ashamed of being the last to awaken, he went to his horse, smoothed the hair on his back, and put the blanket in place. He saddled swiftly and from long habit drew his rifle from the scabbard.

He started to return it, to settle it more securely in place, but something held his hand. What was wrong? He glanced quickly around, but nobody seemed to be watching.

Then he knew. It was his rifle. The weight was wrong.

When a man has lived with guns all his life and with one rifle for a good part of it, he knows the weight and feel of it. Quickly, his horse concealing him from the others, he checked the magazine. It was empty. He worked the lever on his rifle. The barrel was empty, too.

Somebody had deliberately emptied his rifle while he slept!

Swiftly, he shucked cartridges from his belt and reloaded. He was just putting the rifle in the scabbard when Gavin appeared. "Everything all right? We're about to move out."

"I'm ready. I fell asleep over there; first time I've been caught napping in a long time." He smiled pleasantly. "But I'm awake now. Let's go!"

Gavin walked to his horse, and Orrin Sackett swung into the saddle.

Somebody wanted him defenseless. Who? Why? It could hardly be Logan Sackett's enemies, whoever they were. They were over a thousand miles away. Or were they?

Baptiste started the cart moving at a trot. The horse seemed fit enough to go all day.

Avoiding Gavin, Orrin rode wide of the cart, sometimes in advance, scouting, sometimes falling back. He rode warily, his eyes seeking out every bit of cover.

Why unload his rifle unless it was expected that he would need it at once? He thought suddenly of his pistol. He checked it. All secure, loaded, and ready. But, of course, there had been no way they could get to that.

Off to their right, only a short distance away, was the Red River with its thousands of windings through the low hills and between its green banks. Elm, box elder, occasional cottonwood, and much chokecherry or pussywillow crowded the banks and for about a quarter of a mile to a hundred yards on either side.

On the left and over a mile away, another line of trees marked another stream. He mentioned it to Baptiste.

"Wild Rice Creek," he said, "he flows into Red." He pointed with his whip in the direction they were traveling. "Not far."

"And the Sheyenne?"

"Far off—westward. He comes nearer." Baptiste pointed again with his whip to the north. "He comes to marry with Red. You see. Tomorrow, you see."

He rode on ahead, skirting a clump of trees, pausing briefly to let his horse drink at a small creek. He could hear the awful creaking and groaning of the wooden axle of the cart and occasionally a shout from Baptiste.

He listened, hearing the rustle of water in the creek, the scratching of a bird in the leaves, the whisper of the wind through the branches. Quiet sounds, the sounds of stillness, the sound of the woods when they are alone.

His horse, satisfied at last, lifted his dripping muzzle from the cool water, looking about, ears pricked. A drop or two of water fell from his lips. Then, of his own volition, he started on.

Orrin turned his mount suddenly and walked him downstream in the water, then went out on the bank and wove a careful way through a clump of trees, pausing before emerging into the sunlight.

He could see the cart afar off, perhaps a half mile. Suddenly, his horse's head lifted sharply, ears pricked. Orrin shucked his rifle and looked carefully about. Then he saw them.

Two men hunkered down, watching the cart. They were a good twenty yards off, and it was not the Stampers. These were strangers. One wore a black coat, the other a buckskin hunting jacket. Both had rifles.

Orrin stroked the horse's neck, speaking quietly to him, watching. The last thing he wanted now was to precipitate trouble, and what he needed most was information.

One of them started to lift his rifle, and Orrin slid his from the scabbard, but the other man put a hand on the other man's rifle and pushed it down. What he said, Orrin did not know, but they both withdrew into the brush. He waited, listening. After a short interval, he heard a distant sound of horse's hoofs, then silence. He rode back to the cart.

Kyle Gavin rode to meet him. "See anything?"

"There's been somebody around. Travelers, most likely."

How far could he trust Gavin? After all, he knew nothing about the man, and *somebody* had unloaded his rifle, which could have gotten him killed.

Had that somebody been expecting an attack? Perhaps by the two men? Was it his absence from the cart that caused the men to withdraw? Perhaps it was he they wished to kill, and if he was not present—?

Toward sundown, the wind began to pick up again. He scouted on ahead, watching for tracks, using cover. They crossed the Wild Rice, skirted a small settlement, and camped near the crest of a hill away from the river, to be at least partly free from mosquitoes.

Before daybreak, they moved on and by noon reached Georgetown.

"The *International?* She's tied to the bank about twenty mile downstream," a man informed them. "Water's too low here an' there. Wasn't much of a melt this year, so water's low."

The man peered at Orrin. "Name wouldn't be Sackett, would it? There was a feller around askin' after you. Least you come up to what he described. The way he made it out, you was a mighty mean man."

"Me?" Orrin widened his eyes. "I'm a reasonably mild man. Just a tall boy from Tennessee, that's all!"

"Tennessee? Ain't that where they make the good corn liquor? Folks tell me it's the finest whiskey in the world if it's aged proper."

"Kentucky, Tennessee, the Carolinas, they all have good corn whiskey, but as to age, I had a friend down in the Dark Corner who made first-rate whiskey, but he didn't hold much with aging. He said he kept some of it a full week and couldn't see any difference!"

There was a pause, and Orrin asked, "That man who was asking after me? Is he still around?"

"Ain't seen him in a couple of days. A big, tall man with a buckskin huntin' jacket."

"If you see him again," Orrin said mildly, "just tell him Sackett's in town, and if he's got any business with him, to hurry it up because Sackett can't afford to waste around waitin' for him."

"Mister, if I ain't mistaken, that man had killin' on his mind. Least that was the way it sounded."

"Of course. You tell him it's all right now. The frost is out of the ground."

"Frost? What's that got to do with it?"

Orrin smiled pleasantly. "Don't you see? It would be hard to dig a grave for him if the ground were still frozen, but we've had mild weather, and I reckon the digging would be right easy!"

Chapter IX

A tall man in a buckskin jacket? Could he have been one of the two men who were watching the cart?

Georgetown was little more than a cluster of shacks and log houses close to the river. Orrin Sackett wanted no trouble, but if trouble was to come, he preferred it here, now.

He walked the street, alert for a sight of the man in the buckskin jacket, but he saw him nowhere. The stores, he noticed, were well stocked, and it struck him that instead of waiting until he reached Pembina or Fort Garry, he might stock up here. There was a good chance that Riel or someone buying for the Canadian army would have bought out the stores.

For that matter, why not try to buy the Red River cart from Baptiste? Or to hire him to drive? Usually, he had learned, in the long caravans of carts, one driver took care of three carts, and he planned to have but two.

Transporting horses or carts on the *International* was no new thing, so arrangements were quickly made. In the store, he bought the staples he would need. Flour, bacon, beans, dried apples, coffee, tea, and several cases of hardtack, similiar to the Bent's Hard-Water Crackers he had enjoyed as a boy.

He purchased powder, shot and cartridges as well, and four extra rifles.

"Better cache them good," the storekeeper advised. "Louis Riel needs all the guns he can get."

"Do you think there will be a shooting war?" Orrin asked.

The storekeeper shrugged. "Not if Riel can help it. I've done business with him, with his pa, too. They was always reasonable folks, but from what the newcomers are saying, they've got an idea back East that he's leading a rebellion, and they want to hang him."

Outside on the street, Orrin took a quick look around for the buckskin-shirted man but also for anyone else who might seem too interested or too disinterested.

He was worried, and not about what might happen here but what could happen to the north. Tell and Tyrel were depending on him not only for food and ammunition but for additional help, and the last thing he wanted was to get into the midst of a shooting fight in which he had no stake.

The way to stay out of trouble was to avoid the places where trouble was.

When a difficulty develops, unless one can help, it was far better to get away from the area and leave it to those whose business it was to handle such things.

Despite the wisdom of staying out of trouble, his route led right through the middle of it. The best thing he could do would be to get in and out as rapidly as possible.

He looked around the store, buying blankets, a couple of spare ground sheets, odds and ends that would be found useful on the way west where one could buy little or nothing. That was all right. All the Sacketts were used to "making do." It had been their way of life.

"Old Barnabas would enjoy this," he thought suddenly, and said it aloud, not thinking.

"Hey? What's that?"

Orrin smiled. "Just thinking about an ancestor of mine. Came over from England many a year ago, but he was always going west."

"Mine, too," the storekeeper said. "My grandpa left a mighty good farm and a comfortable business. Just sold out and pulled out. Pioneering was in the blood. I guess."

Orrin agreed. "I've got it, too," he admitted. "I'm a lawyer, and I've no business even being here."

"Well, luck to you." The storekeeper looked up. "You goin' west? To the gold fields, maybe?"

"That's right."

The storekeeper shook his head. "I'll talk to Jen about it. That there western country—well, I'd like to see it. I surely would. Wild country, they say, with mountains covered with snow, deep canyons—"

"I'll send my cart around for this," Orrin said.

"Better get you another cart. You got a load here. You got enough for two carts. I've got one I'll let you have reasonable, and a good, steady horse with it."

"The way you talk," Orrin said, "you may need it yourself."

"Up to Jen. I'll talk to her. But maybe—Jenny's got the feelin', too. I seen her lookin' off to the horizon now and again. After all, we was westerin' when we come here." He waved a hand. "Don't worry about the cart. I got a good man can build me one. I'll sell you cart, horse, and harness reasonable. When I come west— well, we may meet up sometime."

"Thanks." Orrin held out his hand. "That's decent of you. If you don't see me, and you hear the name of Sackett, you just go to them and tell him you were friendly to Orrin Sackett. You won't need more than that."

He returned to the street and walked back to the hotel. Baptiste was loaded and standing by his horse.

"You ever been to British Columbia, Baptiste?"

"I dream of it. But it is for young men. I am no longer young."

"It is for men, Baptiste, and you are a man. I have another cart. Will you get it for me?"

"I will. But British Columbia? He iss far off, I t'ink."

"We will cross the wide plains, Baptiste, and follow strange rivers until they are no more. Then we shall climb mountains. It will be cold, hard, and dangerous.

67

You know what the western lands are like, and it is never easy."

Devnet Molrone came out on the street with Mary McCann. "Do we start so soon?"

"It is twenty miles, they say. We will have to hurry."

He glanced up the street. There was a tall man standing there, a tall man in a buckskin coat. Across the street, seated on a bench, was a man in a black coat. He smiled; it was so obvious.

"What is it?" Devnet asked.

"What?" He glanced at her. "Oh? Nothing, I was just—"

"You looked so stern there for a moment, and then almost amused. Somehow—"

"It is nothing," he replied. "It is just that some patterns are so familiar. The men who use them do not seem to realize the same methods have been used for centuries. Each seems to think he invented it."

"I don't believe I understand."

He leaned on the wagon. "Miss Molrone? Do you see those two men up the street? For some reason, they wish me harm. They have followed us here. When I go up the street, as they know I must, the man in the buckskin jacket will start trouble, somehow. Then, when he makes a move to draw a gun, the man across the street in the black coat will try to kill me."

"You're mad!" She stared at him. "That's utterly preposterous! People don't do such things."

"Not so often here as further south, nor so often where we are going. Nevertheless, it does happen. Trial by combat, Miss Molrone, has been a way of life since the beginning of time. A savage way, I'll admit, and dying out. But it is still with us."

"But that's ridiculous! Those two men—why, I saw one of them talking to Mr. Gavin just this morning!"

She turned to look at him. "You do not seem the type, somehow. You're so much the southern gentleman. I just—"

He smiled again. "Southern gentleman? It's just the hat and maybe the fact that I trim my moustache. I grew up in the mountains, ma'am, a-fightin' an' a-feudin', and I cut my western teeth roundin' up wild cows. I've been up the hill and over the mountain, as we Sacketts say."

"But you're a lawyer!"

"Yes, ma'am, and respectful of the law, only if one is to settle difficulties in court, it must be agreeable to both parties. I suspect those gentlemen up the street have already selected their twelve jurymen, and they are in the chambers of their pistols.

"Now," he said, "I must let them present their case, and I am wondering if they have become familiar with a new tactic the boys invented down Texas way?

"We will have to hope they have not heard of it." He unbuttoned his coat. "Miss Molrone, ma'am, would you mind going inside?"

"I will not! Besides, if what you say is true, it's not fair! There are two of them!"

"Please. Do go inside. I know where my bullets are going, but I don't know about theirs."

"Here—what is this?" It was Gavin. "What's going on?"

"It's those men up there. Mr. Sackett believes they will try to kill him."

"*Two* men? I see but one."

"The man in the black coat. Mr. Sackett believes when trouble develops with the one, the other will kill him."

Kyle Gavin's features showed nothing. "Oh? I scarcely think—"

"Gavin? Will you take Miss Molrone inside? I wish to ask that man why he has been following us. If there is anything he wants, I am sure he can have it. There's no need to go skulking about in the brush."

"Following us? I wasn't aware—"

"Perhaps not. I was aware."

"But *two* men? Surely, if you know there are two, or

69

believe there are, I cannot see why you would walk into the trap."

Orrin shrugged a shoulder. "If one knows, it ceases to be a trap. And to an extent the situation is reversed. But that's the lawyer in me. I talk too much."

He turned to Devnet again. "And, Miss Molrone, do let Mr. Gavin take you inside. And please? Stay close to him, for my sake?"

Gavin glanced around. "Now what's that mean?"

"We want her to be safe, do we not?" Orrin's expression was bland.

"If there's a shooting here," Gavin warned, "you will be arrested. The Canadian—"

"We are still in Dakota Territory," Orrin reminded him. "Now will you take Miss Molrone inside?"

"He's right, miss," Mary McCann said. "When lead starts to flyin', anybody can get shot."

The tall man in the buckskin jacket leaned lazily against an awning post. The man opposite in the black coat was reading a newspaper.

Orrin Sackett did not walk toward the man in the buckskin coat, and he did not walk up the middle of the street. He started as if to do one or the other, then switched to the boardwalk that would bring him up behind the man in the black coat.

The tall man straightened suddenly, uncertain as to his move, and in that moment Orrin was behind the man with the newspaper, who had started to turn.

"Sit still now," Orrin warned, "and hang on to that paper. You drop it, and I'll kill you."

The man clutched the paper with both hands. "See here, I don't know what—"

"All right!" Orrin's voice rang clearly in the narrow street. "Unbuckle your gun and let it fall." He was speaking to the man across the street. "Easy now! I don't want to have to kill you."

"Hey? What's this all about?" The man in the buckskin coat rested one hand on his buckle. "What's going on?"

"Nothing, if you unbuckle that belt, nice and easy, and then let it fall."

The man across the street could not even see if Sackett had drawn his gun since he was standing directly behind the man with the newspaper.

The man with the newspaper said, "Better do what he says, Cougar. There's always another day."

Slowly, carefully, Cougar unbuckled his belt and let the gun slip to the ground along with belt and holster.

"Now walk away four steps to your left and stop." Orrin reached down and slipped the seated man's gun from its holster, then a derringer from a vest pocket. He gave the man a quick, expert frisk.

"Fold your paper and put it in your coat pocket," he suggested, "then walk over and join your friend."

As the man walked, Orrin moved across the street behind him and gathered up the gun belt and slung it over his shoulder. "Sit down, boys. Right on the edge of the boardwalk. We might as well be comfortable."

"What's going on?" Cougar demanded. "I don't even know this gent."

Orrin smiled. "You seemed to know each other pretty well when I saw you out in the brush today. I had you under my rifle several times out there, and I was tempted, gentlemen, tempted."

"We was just wonderin' where you was goin'," Cougar said.

"You could have asked us," Orrin said mildly. "No use to skulk in the brush and maybe get mistaken for a Sioux."

"We was just curious"—Cougar's eyes were bright with malice—"especially since you got no reason to go west no more."

Orrin's expression did not change, but within him something went cold and empty. "What's that mean?"

"Them others, with the cows. They're gone. Wiped out. Herd's gone, all of them massacred by the Sioux."

"That's right," the man in the black suit said. "We

71

rode over the ground. The Sioux stampeded buffalo into them an' then follered the buffalo. We seen where a couple of bodies was trampled into prairie, an' gear all over everywhere. They're dead—killed—wiped out."

Chapter X

Orrin's expression did not change. Their faces were sullenly malicious. Cougar hooked his thumbs in his belt. "You lost 'em all," he said, "your family and the cows. The Sioux wiped 'em out. You got nothin' left."

He smiled. It was not easy, but he did it. Were they lying? He wanted to believe it, but he doubted they were.

"They was comin' north," Cougar said. "God knows how they got that far, but they was west of the Turtle Mountains, between there an' the Souris River, when the buffalo stampede hit 'em."

"You saw the bodies?"

"No, I never seen 'em. Hell, there wasn't nothing left. You ever seen a buffalo stampede? Must have been three or four thousand of them.

"We seen some bodies trampled into the torn-up ground. We seen scattered stuff, torn clothing, a busted rifle. Whatever was left the Injuns took, but it can't have been much. And the cattle was scattered to hell and gone!"

Once started, Cougar seemed minded to talk, and Orrin kept still. "There was a little creek comes along there. Don't amount to much, but this time of year there might be water enough for a herd. Anyway, they was in there on a small slope to catch what wind there was because of the skeeters.

"Them Sioux, they'd prob'ly been follerin' them for days, watching for it to be right, and they sure did make it work."

"Why were you following me?"

Cougar shrugged insolently. "Just seen you, wondered what you was doin', then heard your name was Sackett. Figured to tell you what happened."

"All right," Orrin replied, "I'll leave your guns down at the store. But stay off my trail. If I catch you following me, you'd better make your fight because I will."

Abruptly, he turned and walked back to the hotel. Gavin was waiting with Mary McCann and Devnet. "What happened?" he asked.

As briefly as possible, he explained. When he had finished, Devnet said, "Then you won't be going west? You'll stop here?"

"I'll go west, ma'am, and if there's no other way, and you're mindful to travel along, I'll take you and Mrs. McCann. It will be rough, and you won't travel fast, but you can come."

"No," Devnet said, "we'll go to Carlton. We will find a way. But thank you." She paused. "But why will you go now? Everything is gone, finished."

"No, ma'am. Those cattle were stampeded, not killed. I'll round up what I can of them and go on west. If I can find anything left of my brothers, they'll have decent burial, and I'll read from the book over them.

"If not, they'll lie out there with their blood fed into the grass. Ma'am, neither of those boys would feel too lonely out there, for there's Indian blood in that grass. Good men died before them, and there's mighty few western trails that don't have a Sackett buried somewhere along the route. You don't build a country like this on sweat alone, ma'am."

"But there are Indians! And those cattle will be scattered for miles!"

"Yes, ma'am. I'll buy me some extra horses, and if I can find a man or two to help, I'll do it. We started to deliver a herd to the mines, and there's a Sackett yonder who's needful of our help. I reckon I'll go, ma'am, and if it be that I don't make it, well, there's more Sacketts where we come from."

The track lay along the Dakota side of the Red, and they moved at a good pace. Accustomed through long practice, the second horse followed the first cart, driven by Baptiste, without a driver. The afternoon waned, and the lead cart moved faster.

Orrin Sackett drew up to look back along the trail. He saw nothing, no sign of pursuit, no dust. His mount seemed nervous and eager to be off, so he turned and once more began following the carts, although his horse, without any urging, rapidly overtook them.

The carts were moving at a fast trot, and Batpiste kept looking around at the sky on all sides. "How far?" Orrin called out.

"Soon!" Baptiste replied.

The women rode in the carts, resting on the bedrolls and sacks of gear and equipment.

Kyle Gavin, seemingly indisposed to conversation, had ridden on ahead.

Again and again, Orrin looked about, watching the terrain. He was not about to trust Cougar or his companion, and he had neglected to find out who they represented or why they had an interest in him. Not that they showed any indication of being willing to tell him.

Suddenly, the old man yelled at him, gesturing. At the same time, he heard a long, weird moan rise from around or behind him. He had only time to reach up and pull down the mosquito netting from the brim of his hat, and then they were all about him.

He had seen mosquitoes before but nothing like this. They settled on the horse, five and six deep. Again and again, he swept them away, crushing many at a blow, sweeping others away only to have them return in thousands. Suddenly, ahead of them and through the leaves, they saw lights and a gleam of white. It was the *International!* The gangway was down, but there was no one in sight. Without hesitation, they drove aboard, and the women scrambled from the carts and rushed inside.

Kyle Gavin disappeared also, but Orrin remained

behind, covering the horses with fly nets that helped only to a limited degree. Some deck hands appeared, and the gangway was hoisted inboard, and with a great amount of puffing, threshing, and groaning the *International* moved from the bank and started downstream.

To eat supper was impossible. Mosquitoes drowned themselves in the coffee, buried themselves in the melting butter, crawled into the ears and the eyes. Devnet Molrone and Mary McCann had already given up and disappeared. Orrin followed.

In his small stateroom, there were mosquitoes, too. He succeeded in driving many outside by waving a towel, then got under the netting on his bunk. Dead tired, he slept, awakening in the cool of morning to find no mosquitoes about.

Shaving was all but impossible, but he worried through it, swearing more than a little. From the porthole he could see green banks sliding past.

After a while, in a clean shirt, he emerged on deck. From the pilot he learned the *International* was one hundred and thirty-odd feet long but drew only two feet of water. There were few straight stretches on the river, for it persisted in a fantastic series of S curves that seemed without end. Some of the curves could barely be negotiated, and the longer Mississippi boats would have had no chance here.

Returning to his cabin after a quick, pleasant breakfast, Orrin checked his guns once more. Soon they would be in the little frontier post of Pembina. He must make new plans now. Without his brothers, he must do what needed to be done alone or with what help he could secure.

Tell and Tyrel gone! His mind refused to accept it.

William Tell Sackett, that older brother of his, the quiet, steady one, always so sure, so strong, so seemingly fearless.

Tyrel, younger than he as he was younger than Tell,

but Tyrel was different, had always been different. And perhaps the best of them all with a gun.

Gone!

No, he'd not accept it, not until he found some tangible evidence of their death. Yet, at the same time, his experience told him the risk they had run, the dangers to be expected, the attraction of such a herd of cattle moving through Sioux country.

Nonetheless, he must plan as though they were gone. He must plan to round up the cattle, scattered though they might be, and deliver them himself.

He would, of course, need help. Baptiste seemed willing to go along, but he was only a cart driver. What he would need would be cowboys or some of the *métis*, who were handy men at anything. They, however, would be busy with Riel and the pending rebellion.

Pembina—he must see what could be done there. And there were a couple of men aboard the *International* who might be interested.

Devnet Molrone did not appear on deck, and Kyle Gavin seemed preoccupied. Orrin walked along the upper deck, watching the shoreline and the river ahead, although rarely could they see the river for more than a few hundred yards, if that far.

Twice he saw deer, once a small herd of buffalo. He saw no Indians.

There were few passengers aboard. Three men and a woman bound for Pembina and a tall, lean young man for Fort Garry. There was also a portly, middle-aged man in a tweed suit.

"This Riel," the latter said distastefully, "who does he think he is? How dare he? He's nothing but a bloody savage!"

"I understood he'd studied for the priesthood," the young man protested, "and worked for some paper in Montreal or somewhere."

"Balderdash! The man's an aborigine! Why, he's part Indian! Everybody knows that!"

"One-eighth," the young man said.

"No matter. Who does he think he is?"

"From what I hear," Orrin suggested mildly, "he simply stepped in to provide a government where there was none."

"Balderdash! The man's an egotistical fool! Well," he said finally, "no need to bother about him. The army will be here soon, and they'll hang him. Hang him, I say!"

The young man looked over at Orrin and shrugged. After a bit, he walked forward with him. "A man of definite opinions," Orrin said mildly.

"I know little enough about Riel except some poetry of his that I've read. Not bad at all, not bad. But he seems a reasonable man."

"If they give him time," Orrin commented. "It would seem some at least have already made up their minds."

"You're headed west, I hear?"

"British Columbia, but first I've got to round up some cattle and find, if I can, the bodies of my brothers, who are said to have been killed in a stampede."

"Dash it all! I am sorry! I heard something to that effect." He glanced at Orrin. "Going to the gold fields?"

"Eventually, if we get the cattle."

"I would take it as a favor if you permitted me to come along."

"You?" Orrin glanced at him. "I will carry no excess baggage. If you come with me, you will work and be paid for it. You will ride, round up cattle and drive them, and if necessary, fight Indians."

"I'm your man. It sounds like great fun."

"It won't be. It is brutally hard work, and a good chance to be killed."

"I understand Miss Molrone is going with you?"

So that was it? "She may change her mind. Right now she is headed for Carlton House and may go no further. If it is she whom you're interested in, I would suggest you go to Carlton House."

Pembina would soon be showing up around a bend.

Once there, he could begin recruiting, but instead of the two men he had hoped to get, now he would need at least four and preferably more. This young man—what was his name? He might prove to be just the man he needed.

Kyle Gavin came forward to stand beside him, watching the blunt bow part the river waters. Huge elms hung over the river, extending limbs out from either side until they almost met above the river. Here and there along the banks were clumps of willow, some grown into trees of some size.

"Dev—, I mean Miss Molrone tells me you've had bad news? About your brothers, I mean?"

"Yes, the man called Cougar told me they were dead. That they had been killed. I'll believe that when I see it."

"I *am* sorry! I must—well, I have to admit I heard the same story, but I just hadn't—I mean, I couldn't bring myself to tell you."

Orrin glanced at Gavin, his eyes cool. "I prefer to know such things. The sooner the better."

"You're still going west?"

"Why not? I still have a herd to deliver. Their death, if dead they are, changes nothing in that sense."

"But your cattle are gone! Scattered to the winds, and probably many of them have been killed. What can you do?"

"That we will see, Mr. Gavin. A cousin of mine is waiting for the delivery of those cattle. He will not be disappointed."

Gavin stared at him in obvious disbelief. "But you don't seem to understand! You're over two thousand miles from there! You have no cattle! You have nobody to help! The same Sioux who killed your brothers will be waiting for you, and further west there are Blackfeet! You don't have a chance!

"Even," he added, "if Riel does not requisition your carts and supplies. And if he does not demand them, the army certainly will. Such things are in short supply."

"We will manage."

Suddenly, there was a blast from the whistle. Orrin Sackett turned, pulling his hat brim down.

Pembina was just ahead.

Chapter XI

Pembina had little to offer. A customhouse, a trade store, and a scattering of cabins. The oldest settlement around, its fortunes had varied with travel and the fur trade, but now Fort Garry and the village of Winnipeg were attracting settlers that might otherwise have been drawn to Pembina.

Orrin Sackett wasted no time, for the *International* would be there for but a short stay. He walked up to the trading post and looked around quickly.

Only a few men were present, at least two of whom he immediately catalogued as drunks. He started to turn away when he stopped and looked again at the man at the end of the bar. He had his hat pushed back, and an impudent grin touched his lips. "Howdy!" he said. "You all still rustlin' for men?"

"How are you, Shorty? Yes, I am." He paused. "You travel fast."

"It's a mighty poor horse that ain't faster'n that steamboat, what with all the curves in that river. I beat you by a whole day." Shorty emptied his glass. "Word gets around that you won't be needin' any hands. They say your cattle were stampeded and your brothers killed. They say you're wiped out."

Orrin pushed his hat back. He glanced at the bartender. "A beer," he said, "and give Shorty whatever he's drinking."

He waited for the beer, took a swallow, and then said, "I never seen a herd so scattered that a man couldn't round up some of them, and as for Tell and Tyrel, they don't kill very easy. I've seen 'em shot at,

81

I've seen 'em wounded, I've seen them days without food or water, and somehow they always came through.

"Regardless, we gave our word to deliver cattle, and deliver them I will if I have to round up a herd of buffalo and drive them through.

"I've got just one man, Shorty, an' old cart driver named Baptiste. We've got two cartloads of grub an' gear, and I'm rustling for men and horses.

"Out west there, they've got some mighty mean Sioux, some meaner Blackfeet, and some grizzlies that will stand higher than a horse and heavier than a bull. They've got mountains where nobody ever drove a cow critter before, and there may be some men along the trail who'd like to stop us. What d'you say?"

"Sounds like my kind of a deal." Shorty tossed off his drink. "Finish your beer. I know a man who's got some horses."

Two hours later, Orrin owned six new horses. Shorty stood back and watched him, an amused smile on his face. Orrin passed by dozens of horses to choose the six he finally bought.

"You done yourself proud," Shorty said. "You got yourself six of the best. But you get to roundin' up stock on the plains, and six horses won't last even two men no time at all."

"We'll have more. What I need right now is men."

"Tough. Usually, you could find all you wanted. These *métis* ain't cowpunchers by a long shot, but they can ride, and they can shoot, and you find quite a few who are fair hands with a rope. And they're workers, every durned one of them."

The steamboat whistled. "Shorty? You want to meet me in Fort Garry with these horses?"

"Surest thing you know. But you watch your step. That's a mighty touchy situation there."

He had no doubt of it, yet there was nothing to do but to go ahead and cope with the situations as they occurred.

He could not make himself believe that Tell and

Tyrel were dead. If not dead, they might be lying somewhere, injured and suffering. Or they might be prisoners of the Sioux.

He made the *International* just as they were taking in the gangway.

Devnet met him on the upper deck. "It isn't far now, is it?" she asked.

"A few more hours. You are going to Fort Carlton?"

"Of course."

"Is Mrs. McCann going with you?"

"I think not. I do not know her well, you know. We just met while traveling, and all I know is that she wishes to go west, all the way to the Pacific."

"You should have no trouble."

She turned to him suddenly. "I am sorry about your brothers, so very sorry. Were you so very close?"

"We had our differences, but they never amounted to much. Yes, we were close. I left my law practice to help them."

"What will you do now?"

"Find their bodies, if possible, bury them, and then round up the cattle and go on west." He paused. "But I cannot believe they are dead. They were both so strong, so alive. They were survivors. They'd been through a lot."

He hesitated, then said, "Miss Molrone, I—"

"My friends call me Nettie. It is easier to say than Devnet."

"All right, Nettie. What will you do if you learn nothing of your brother at Carlton?"

"Go on west, I presume. He has to be there."

"You must realize there is no regular mode of travel to the west, only occasional groups of travelers. Someday there will be a railroad. They are talking of it now, and since this Riel trouble, I imagine there will be a serious effort made, but that's years away."

"I have to go—somehow."

"We will not be going by way of Carlton but will be going west from Fort Ellice. We will follow the Qu'Appelle River, more or less. If you could join us—of course, it will be rough, sleeping on the ground and all that."

"I could do it."

They talked the morning away but saw nothing of Kyle Gavin. Before the noontime meal, Mary McCann came up to join them. She said little, had blunt but not unattractive features, and Orrin noticed her hands showed evidence of much hard work.

Occasionally, now, there were breaks in the wall of trees on either bank, and they could catch glimpses of meadows and in one case of a plowed field. The country was very flat, and the river wound slowly through it They saw many ducks and an occasional hawk.

A dozen men armed with rifles, whom he took to be *métis,* waited on the landing. One of them came forward as the carts were being driven ashore. His name, he said, was Lepine.

"I am Orrin Sackett."

Lepine nodded. "We have heard of you." He gestured to the carts. "These will be confiscated."

Briefly, Orrin explained. Lepine shrugged. "It will be up to Louis. He will decide."

It was arranged for him to be conducted to the fort where Riel had taken up his residence.

Riel came into the room wearing a black frock coat, vest and trousers, and moccasins, as did nearly everyone. He had quick, intelligent eyes, a broad forehead, and a shock of black hair.

He listened, his eyes roaming around the room, as Orrin explained. At the end, he nodded. "Of course. We will release your goods. I have heard of the attack you mention."

"And my brothers? Were they killed?"

"What we heard was little enough. There was a stampede, an attempt to scatter the cattle so the Sioux could take them when they wished.

"There was some fighting, which would imply somebody survived the stampede. The Sioux claim to have lost no one, but one of my men, who was in their camp shortly after, learned there were some losses, and the Sioux had but one fresh scalp that he saw."

He glanced at Orrin. "You must give me your word the rifles will not be used against me, nor the supplies given to those who consider themselves my enemies."

His restless eyes kept moving about the room. Suddenly, he asked, "How many men do you have?"

"Two—now. A cart driver named Baptiste—"

Riel smiled. "I know him. A good old man." He looked around at Orrin. "But only two? What can you do?"

"I hope to find more."

"Well"—he shook his head doubtfully—"you have a problem." He waved a hand. "Go! It is all right! You shall have your carts. I want trouble with no one. I began all this because I wanted peace. There were surveyors coming on our land, and I was afraid there would be a shooting."

Orrin turned to the door, and his hand was on the latch when Riel spoke again. "Wait! There is a man, an American like yourself. He is in jail here. I think he is a good man."

"In jail for what?"

"Fighting."

Orrin smiled. "All right. I will talk to him."

"If you hire him, the case will be dismissed." Riel smiled slyly, his eyes twinkling. "Just take him away from here. It needed four of my men to get him locked up."

Lepine unlocked the cell, and a man got up from the straw. He was at least two inches taller than Orrin's six feet and four inches but leaner. He had a handlebar moustache and a stubble of beard. One eye was black, fading to blue and yellow, and his knuckles were skinned.

"You want a job?" Orrin said.

"I want to get out of here."

"You take the job, you get out. Otherwise, they'll throw the key away."

"Don't look like I have much choice." He stared at Orrin. "What kind of a job is this, anyway?"

"Rounding up cattle stampeded by buffalo. It's in Sioux country."

"Hell, I'd rather stay in jail. They gotta let me out sometime."

He was watching Orrin, and suddenly he said, "What's your name, mister?" He paused. "It wouldn't be Sackett, would it?"

"It would. I am Orrin Sackett."

"I'll be damned! They call me Highpockets Haney. I thought you had the mark on you. You Sacketts all seem cut to the same pattern, sort of. I served in the army with a Sackett named William Tell."

"My brother."

"I'll be damned! All right, you got yourself a boy. On'y you got to get me a *wee*pon. They done taken my rifle gun an' my pistol."

A burly *métis,* sitting on a log with a rifle across his knees, looked up as they came out. "Take heem! Take heem far! He geef me a leep!" He touched his lip with tender fingers.

"Hell," Haney said, "look at the eye you gave me!"

"What we fight about?"

Haney chuckled. "You expect *m*e to remember? More'n likely I wondered whether you was as tough as you looked." He chuckled again. "You're tougher!"

Shorty was at the customhouse with the six horses. He led the way to a place back from the river and on a grassy hillside under the spreading branches of some old trees. "Camped here before," he explained.

He watched Baptiste come up the rise with the two carts. "Ain't much of an outfit, but it's a start," he suggested. "We'll need at least two more men, and we should have six."

"We'll just have to look around," Orrin said, "but there's three of us now."

The next man was a volunteer. He approached Shorty, who was having a beer. "You look like a rider," he suggested. "I'm another, and I'm broke and rustlin' work."

His name was Charlie Fleming, and he was from Arkansas, he said. He had two horses of his own and knew where there were four more to be had.

"That's it," Orrin told them. "We'll move out tomorrow. The first thing is to find where that stampede took place and hunt for my brothers, or their bodies."

"You won't find much," Fleming said. "Not after a stampede. I lost a friend thataway, and all we found was his boot heels and some buttons. By the time several hundred head of buffalo run over you, there isn't much to find."

"We'll look," Haney said. "Tell Sackett was the best friend I ever had. We were in the Sixth Cavalry together."

Orrin walked back to the hotel. Studiously, he had avoided any thought of his brothers. His job was to get an outfit. When the time came to look, that would be another thing.

Three men riding and one on the carts. Four men riding, counting himself. It was too few, and he should have about ten more horses. Rounding up scattered cattle, if any were left, would be rough on the riding stock.

The first person he saw at the hotel was Nettie Molrone. "Oh, Mr. Sackett! I'm so glad to see you! I'm leaving in the morning for Fort Carlton!"

"Who's taking you?"

"I'm going with a group. Mrs. McCann is going, and there will be another lady whose husband is there. There are six trappers, Mr. Taylor from the Hudson's Bay Company, and Kyle Gavin."

"I wish you luck," he said. His expression was a little sour, and she noticed it. "I mean, I really do," he added. "I'll be leaving tomorrow, too."

"I know. I mean, Mr. Gavin said he believed you were leaving. He doesn't think you'll have much luck."

"We'll see." He hesitated, then said, "I hope you

find your brother and that everything goes well for you. Remember, we'll be miles to the south of you, and once we get the cattle, we'll be driving west. We'll follow the South Saskatchewan."

"But aren't the cattle down in Dakota?"

"On the border," he said. "We'll need several days to round them up."

He was in his room and combing his hair before going down to dinner when the thought struck him. How did Kyle Gavin know he was leaving?

He didn't even have his outfit yet, not the men or stock he needed.

Just a surmise, probably. A lucky guess.

Chapter XII

The morning was clear and bright with only a few scattered clouds. The wind sent ripples through the vast sea of grass before them, but the sound of it was lost in the screech and groan of the carts, which were entirely of oak and ungreased.

Highpockets Haney rode up beside Orrin. "You got your work cut out for you, Sackett," he said. "You ever rounded up cattle scattered by a buffalo stampede? They're likely to be scattered to hell an' gone."

"It won't be easy."

"We'll be workin' alone most of the time, just the way the Injuns like it."

"We'll work in pairs," Orrin suggested. "Takes less time to bunch them. If trouble comes, use your own judgment. Fight if that's necessary, but run if you can, just so long as you run together. I don't want any man left alone unless he's already dead."

Now he left them, riding out at least a mile in advance of the carts and the other riders. Since the news had come, there had been no time to be alone, no time to mourn, no time to think, only time for the immediate business, and first things must come first.

They had started to drive cattle to the gold fields because Logan Sackett had promised it. Therefore the job must be continued. Logan was still in trouble, and a Sackett had given his word.

Rumor had it his brothers were dead. He did not believe it, yet it could be. Men died every day, and his brothers were no more immune than their father had been.

It was his mission now to go to the area, accept the risks it entailed, round up the cattle if possible, and find and bury the bodies of his brothers.

Feeling sad was a luxury he could not afford at the moment. With resolution, he turned from sadness to the task at hand. Now, with all going forward, he could think, so he rode far out before his small party where he could ride alone.

He was alone, simply with his horse, the sound of his passing, and the wind in the grass.

Tell and Tyrel—gone! That he could not accept, even for the moment. Tell had always been the older brother, strong, quiet, and sure. He had been less talkative, even, than Tyrel, who was himself quiet. He, Orrin, had always been the easy-talking one, taking after the Welsh side of the family.

He remembered the day when Tell, still only a boy, had ridden off to war. They lived in the mountains of Tennessee and had kinfolk fighting for the Confederacy, but Tell had said, "Ma, I'm a goin' to war. I'm goin' to fight for the Union."

"For the Union, son?"

"Yes, ma. It's my bounden duty. Our folks fought to build this country, and I'll not turn my back on it. It's our country, all of it, Not just the South. And there's many a boy in Kentucky and Tennessee feels likewise."

He went in the night, using the old Indian trails, that only mountian folk knew, and somehow he got through to Ohio, and eventually he'd wound up in the Sixth Cavalry. He never said much about the war years, and if he met any kinfolk on the field of battle, he didn't say.

When it was over, he'd gone to fightin' Injuns and then quit the army and joined up with a cattle drive. He'd covered a far stretch of country before their paths crossed again in the western lands. So far as they knew, Tell had not been back to Tennessee, which was surprising because there'd been a girl back yonder that he'd been shinin' up to when the war started.

Tyrel was the youngest but already married and owner of a ranch, part of which his wife brought to him, but which he'd helped to save from renegades in the Land Grant fights. He was better off than any of them. He owned land and stock, but he owed money, and this trip was costing him.

This was wide-open country, yet there were unexpected hollows and valleys, and a man had to keep his wits about him. There were sloughs, small lakes usually surrounded by a thick stand of cattails. The hills were green now; only a few days had made a striking difference. The grass was short but long enough to color the hills with springtime. Wild flowers were everywhere, harebell, silverberry, and blue-eyed grass as well as wild parsley and yellow violet.

Here and there were small herds of antelope, and occasionally they saw a buffalo.

That night by their small fire he warned them again. "This here's Sioux country, and they're first-class fighting men. You got to expect them all the time."

On the third day they killed a buffalo for fresh meat and skinned it out with the meadowlarks calling. Orrin's eyes kept roving, searching, watching, yet a part of his mind was far away, with Nettie Molrone, wondering where she was and how she fared.

Douglas Molrone—he must remember the name and listen for it, yet the gold fields had a way of devouring men, of chewing them up and spitting them out at the ragged ends of the world. It was whiskey and hard work that did them in, standing in cold streams, panning for the elusive gold.

So many times even the best discoveries somehow seemed to come to nothing. Tell had struck it rich in the mountains of Colorado only to have the vein play out. He had taken out a goodly sum, but part of it had gone back into searching for the lost vein. Sometime, somebody would discover it, broken off and shifted by some convulsion of the earth.

In the distance, they could see the flat-looking blue

shadow that was the Turtle Mountains. Not mountains at all but a plateau of rolling country scattered with lakes and pretty meadows among the trees.

The dim trail they were following, probably made by *métis* buffalo hunters, skirted the Turtle Mountains on the north, but Orrin led the way south, skirting the plateau's eastern end and making camp near a slough almost in the shadow of the hills.

"Keep your rifles handy," he advised, "but be damned sure you see what you're shooting at. You boys know as well as I do that some or all of them might come through a stampede. If it takes place at night there'd likely be only two, three men on night herd, and they'd know you can't stop a buffalo stampede."

"So?" Fleming asked.

"It's likely they'd scatter. They'd take out an' run," Haney said. "That's what I'd do. A dead cowhand ain't no good to anybody."

"If my brothers or Cap come through this, they'd more than likely take to the hills. There's water there, and there are hideouts and small game."

They were camped in a small hollow with some low brush around, a few polished granite boulders left by a vanished glacier, and several tall cottonwoods. The slough where they watered their stock was about fifty yards below. Baptiste built a small fire and roasted buffalo steaks. Orrin could not rest but prowled about outside of the hollow, listening for any small sound.

He heard nothing but the expected sounds of the night.

It was very still. To the north loomed the bulk of the plateau; to the west the land fell gradually away into a vast plain, which he suspected was a prehistoric lake bed. Behind him there was a faint rustling of wind in the cottonwood leaves and a low murmur of voices.

Somewhere out in that great silence were his brothers and Cap, alive or dead, and he had to find them.

He walked out a few steps farther, listening. Overhead were the stars, and the sky was very clear. He moved out still farther, haunted by the feeling that something was out there, something vague that he could not quite realize.

He let his eyes move slowly all around the horizon, searching for any hint of a fire. He turned his head this way and that, trying for a smell of smoke.

Nothing!

Were they gone, then? Truly gone? After all, there is a time for each of us.

Faintly, something stirred. His gun came easily into his hand. He waited, listening. There was nothing more.

Some small animal, perhaps.

After a few minutes, he went back to the fire. In the morning, they would continue on to the westward. Then he would climb the plateau and see what he could see from that height. Certainly, he could see farther, and he might detect some movement out there. Also, he should check for tracks.

The trouble was there were, so he had heard, many lakes in the Turtles and no end to available water. It was not as simple as in the desert where waterholes were few.

"Charlie," he suggested, "you take the first watch. Give yourself an hour and a half, then awaken Shorty. The same for you, Shorty, and then call Haney and Haney will call me."

"You t'ink I am too old?" Baptiste asked.

"You have to get up early, anyway, and you'll have to watch the camp tomorrow. You get some sleep now."

Fleming took up his rifle. "Anything else?"

"Don't sit by the fire. Stay out on the edge somewhere."

He unrolled his bed and pulled off his boots, then his gun belt. Shorty was asleep almost as soon as he hit his blankets, and Haney followed suit. Baptiste stirred about a bit, then settled down.

Orrin lay still, listening. The fire had burned down to reddish coals. His six-gun was ready at his hand. He heard a brief stirring outside of camp, then stillness.

Haney touched his shoulder just as his eyes were opening. Haney squatted on his heels. "Quiet," he said, "but there's an uneasy feelin' in the air."

"Everybody asleep?"

"Sure, except maybe that Frenchman. I don't know if he ever sleeps."

Orrin sat up and tugged on his boots. For a moment he waited, listening and looking at the coals. If they were to keep the fire, he must add fuel, but he did not want it to flare up. He slung his gun belt around his hips as he stood up, then moved on cat feet over to the fire and with a stick pushed some of the charcoal into the redder coals. If there was a flare-up, it would be slight.

Moving back into the shadows, he retrieved his rifle, stood it against a tree, and shrugged into a buckskin jacket, then moved out to where the horses were. Their quiet munching indicated there was, for the moment, nothing to suggest trouble.

The stars were still bright overhead, but there were clouds in the northwest. After a circling of the camp, he sat down on a rock in the shadows of a larger one and began to consider the situation.

Except for what he had been told, he had no further evidence that his brothers had not continued on west. Knowing them as he did, he knew nothing would turn them from the way they had chosen. If they had been attacked and killed, he would know it within hours, for the battle site could not be far off.

Yet he must not lose time looking for them. He would look, but he would also round up what cattle he could find. It was likely that the cattle were scattered in bunches, for they would certainly try to find one another, and by this time they would have done so.

Soon he must awaken Baptiste and let him prepare breakfast for an early start, for today they would not only search for his brothers and their riders but would begin gathering cattle, if there were any to be found.

He got up suddenly and moved away, impatient with himself. This, of course, was a family matter and not to be avoided, but he had wasted time, too much time. No man knew how much or how little he had, but there were things that he, Orrin Sackett, wanted to do, wanted to become.

He had been admitted to the bar, had begun a practice of sorts, mixed with some political activity, but not enough of either. He had too much to learn to be losing any time. When this was over, he would get right back to Colorado and try to become the man he wished to be.

He remembered something pa said. Pa quoted it, rather, from a distant relative gone long before. "There's two kinds of people in the world, son, those who wish and those who will. The wishers wish to be rich, they wish to be famous, they wish to own a farm or a fine house or whatever. The ones who will, they don't *wish*, they start out and *do* it. They become what they want to or get what they want. They *will* it."

Well, he wasn't going to be a wisher. He'd been lucky. He'd begun to get himself an education. He'd not gone to school long, as there wasn't a school to go to most of the time. But there'd been books.

Suddenly, he was alert. Something was moving out there. He melded his shadow against a tree, listening. There was no further sound.

Orrin's rifle came up in his two hands, ready for a shot or a blow.

After a minute, with no further sound, he eased back close to where Baptiste lay. The old man was already sitting up, shaking out his boots.

"Somet'ing," he whispered, "somet'ing, he come. He come soon."

Standing back a little, Orrin threw several branches on the fire. It flared up, and he added some heavier wood.

When he stood up again, it was faintly gray. Baptiste was working over the fire, and Orrin went out to where the horses were and saddled his mount.

"Comes a man," Baptiste said. "You see?"

Highpockets Haney stood up on his bed, looking. Orrin walked closer.

Down on the flat, if it could be called that, there was a man, a big man who moved like a bear. He came on slowly, head down, plodding.

Some fifty yards away, he stopped and looked at them. "I'm the Ox," he said. "I'm coming in."

Chapter XIII

Orrin waited, his hands on his hips while the big man lumbered closer. He was huge, not as tall as Orrin's six feet four inches but thicker and wider. He gave off a sense of shocking physical power, to such a degree that Orrin was irritated by it.

A civilized man with some sense of decency and proportion, he bristled at the sight of the man. He had the good sense to realize it was something of the same feeling two stallions must feel when first they met. He had had his share of fights, but he had never *wanted* to hit a man until now.

"All right," Orrin said, "you are called the Ox. What else are you? Who are you?"

The Ox knew who he was facing. He did not know the man or care, but he sensed a rival male beast and welcomed it. He was a creature nature had bred to destroy.

"There was a stampede, buffalo. Everything went with them. Men, horses, cattle, everything. There was nothing I could do."

"Where were you when it happened?"

"Off to one side. I was swinging wide around the herd. They came out of the night like—like an avalanche. And then it was all gone."

"Where's your horse?"

"Gone. He went crazy when the stampede came, and he threw me. He ran away following the herd."

"Get something to eat. You look all in." The trouble was that he did not, and Orrin sat down across the fire

97

from him. Something here was wrong, completely wrong. The Ox did not look done in; he did not look tired or hungry. He had appeared so, coming up the slope from the flat, but no longer. His gun was still in its holster.

Orrin's sense of justice warred with his innate dislike of the man he was watching. He warned himself to dismiss his antagonism and judge fairly.

"Was this the Sackett herd?" he asked.

The big man was eating, not very seriously. A really hungry man did not gulp food, he savored it, he ate slowly. A truly hungry man cannot gulp food because his stomach has shrunk. He is more apt to eat in small bites. The Ox ate as one does who has already eaten his fill, which is a different thing altogether.

"It was. Gilcrist and me, we hired on some time back. The drive was headed west. All gone now, all gone."

"What happened to the Sacketts?"

"Dead, I reckon. They must be dead."

"But if you were off to one side, mightn't they have been, also?"

The Ox squinted his eyes. Orrin suspected he did not like the thought. "Maybe, but I ain't seen them."

"Where have you been since?"

"Hidin' from Injuns. I ain't seen any, but I think it was them started the stampede."

Orrin watched the Ox put down his plate. The man's movements were easy, perfectly controlled. There was much about him that was puzzling. He was, Orrin was sure, a much brighter man than he at first appeared and probably a better-educated one.

Orrin stood up. "All right, boys, as soon as you're through eating, let's move out. Work south and east, and stay together, two by two. I'll ride with Fleming.

"You"—he turned on the Ox, "help Baptiste—and tomorrow we'll start you riding for us."

The Ox started to speak, then turned away obviously irritated.

"Work south and east but not too far east. Anything you find, start this way. We'll try to bunch them on the flat down there."

"That's crazy!" the Ox exclaimed. "They're scattered to hell and gone!"

"Maybe," Orrin agreed, "but we'll find out, won't we?"

It was a long, hard day. Fleming and Orrin worked south and for some time saw nothing. Twice Orrin cut the sign of old Indian travels. Then they came upon three young steers and started them west.

"Take them along, Fleming," Orrin said. "They'll be a start, anyway, and I'll work on south."

"But I think—"

"It's all right," Orrin said blandly.

Fleming, none too pleased, rode off herding his three steers.

Orrin waited until he was some distance off and then turned back. In less than three hundred yards, he found what he had seen a few minutes before, the tracks of two shod horses and a trail obviously made that day. One of the horses had been carrying a very heavy man.

At a point where the trail would have brought them within sight of Orrin's camp, the two riders had suddenly turned south. Orrin followed, swinging along the trail in a wide circle. There, in the shade of some cottonwoods, one of the riders had dropped from the saddle and walked away.

The other rider had gone off to the west, leading a spare horse.

Orrin Sackett glanced off to the east where the rider had taken the spare horse and then turned in the saddle and glanced up at the plateau of the Turtles. "I'd lay a little bet," he muttered aloud.

He rode south, swinging in a wide circle toward the west, and in a little hollow found six head of cattle gathered around a small seep. He moved them out toward the northwest, picking up two more on the way.

By the time he reached the gathering place, there were at least thirty head there, and Fleming was bringing in another.

Throughout the day, they worked, finding more and more of the scattered groups with occasionally a buffalo calf running with them. By sundown, they had gathered nearly three hundred head.

Baptiste had shifted camp farther west by a good five miles, with the Turtle Mountains still looming close on the north. He had a good fire going on some broiled buffalo steaks for all hands as well as more of his beans. He had made sourdough bread, and they ate simply but well.

The Ox was irritable and not talkative. It was obvious things had not gone as he expected. Baptiste was wary, watchful, and kept a gun handy, not trusting the Ox.

"There's a-plenty off to the southwest," Haney told them. "I saw maybe fifty, sixty head in one bunch and glimpsed several other scattered bunches.

"It won't be easy," he added. "They're scattered wide, and there's still a good many buffalo among 'em who will stampede again at the slightest excuse. If they do, most of those damn fool cows will go right along with them."

"We need more help," Orrin suggested, "but tomorrow we'll have the Ox helping us."

"I ain't in no shape to ride," the Ox muttered.

"If you want to eat," Orrin replied, "you'll ride. You can work with me. I think we understand each other mighty well."

The Ox glared but made no comment.

"We may be able to get some help," Shorty suggested. "This country isn't as empty as a body might think. I came on two sets of tracks today, both of them shod horses and none of them our horses."

Orrin knew he had been shying away from the thing that must be done. He had been avoiding the site of the stampede, and he knew why. If Tell and Tyrel were dead, he did not want to know it. Until he actually saw their bodies or some other evidence that proved them dead, he could still delude himself they were alive still.

"Tomorrow I am going over to check their last camp." Orrin glanced at the Ox. "You can show me where it was."

The Ox said nothing, sipping a cup of coffee, and Shorty smiled. "Ain't much to see," he said. "I was over there."

They waited, and he said, "I scouted that country some. The buffalo hit that camp goin' all out, and they just run everything right into the ground. But I don't think anybody was in the camp."

"What?" Orrin turned to stare. "Then where in God's name—?"

"They were with the cattle. They were moving them when the stampede hit them." He glanced at the Ox. "Wasn't that what you said? You were off on the flank?"

"I was." The Ox paused. "It was like I said. They were here, then they were gone, and the cattle with them. I heard one man scream. I've no idea who it was."

"Did you see any Indians?" Orrin asked.

The Ox hesitated. "Can't say I did. I heard whooping. I figured it was Indians, and I lit out."

"Haney, you and Shorty continue the roundup. The Ox and I will go over the site of the stampede before we settle down to rounding up cattle."

Orrin glanced at Baptiste. "You stay with the carts and keep your rifle handy. Any sign of trouble everybody closes in on the carts, do you hear? We need that grub."

It was a quiet night, and before daybreak they were in the saddle. Orrin, with the Ox beside him, rode down toward the site of the stampede.

The Ox turned in his saddle to look at Orrin. "You don't like me much, do you, Sackett?"

"No, I don't."

"When the right time comes, I'll take pleasure in beating your head in," the Ox said.

Orrin smiled. "Don't talk like a fool, man. You couldn't whip one side of me, and away down inside you know it."

The Ox was not amused. "Nobody ever whipped me," he said, "and nobody can."

"Keep that thought. I want you to have it when I prove you wrong."

Orrin drew up, looking over the terrain before them. The shallow valley, if such it might be called, sloped away toward the south. The earth was still torn by charging hoofs. He glanced around, taking in the situation. The Ox stared at it, then looked away. "You know, Ox," Orrin said quietly, "you're a liar. Your whole story is a tissue of lies, from start to finish. Now where's your partner?"

The Ox stared at him, an ugly expression in his eyes. "I don't know what you're talkin' about, but you just called me a liar."

"That's right. I did call you a liar." He put up a hand. "Now don't be a damned fool and go for your gun. I'm a whole lot faster than you and a much better shot, and you'd be dead before you cleared leather.

"You boys bought yourselves a packet, d'you know that? If you're going to try to get away with something, why don't you pick on some greenhorns?"

The Ox was wary. He did not believe Orrin Sackett was faster than he, but neither did he want to be mistaken. It was a simple case. If he was wrong, he was dead.

"My brothers, William Tell and Tyrel, are two of the fastest men alive when it comes to handling six-shooters. I'm only a shade less good.

"Just a moment ago, I had a notion to let you go ahead and draw so I could kill you."

The Ox stared at him. "Then why didn't you if you're so fast?"

Orrin smiled. "Because I'd miss the pleasure of whipping you with my fists," he said. Orrin rested both hands on the pommel of his saddle. "You see, Ox, you've always been big, you've always been strong, you've always been able to either frighten or outmuscle anybody whose trail you crossed. So the truth is, you've never really had to learn to fight. You've never had to get up after being knocked down. You've never had to wipe the blood out of your eyes so you could see enough to keep fighting.

"You're not really a fighter, Ox, you're just a big, abnormally strong man who has had it all his own way for too long."

The Ox smiled. "Maybe I don't have to know how to fight," he said. "I just take hold and *squeeze*, and they scream. You can hear the bones break, Sackett. I will hear yours break."

Orrin looked around again. "Now where were you when the stampede started?"

The Ox pointed across the plain. "Over there. Tyrel Sackett was riding drag. That's why I am sure he is dead."

"What d'you mean?"

"They hit us on the flank, more than halfway back, and there was no way Tyrel could get out of there."

"Then I've misunderstood. I didn't know it was that way." Orrin paused. "What kind of a horse was Tye riding?"

"It was that line-back dun he favored. I remember that because he let Brandy—"

"Who?"

"The kid—Isom Brand was his name. We called him Brandy. He wasn't much. Some farm kid they taken up with. Anyway, I remember Tyrel rode the dun because he let Brandy have that little black."

Orrin was thinking. If Tyrel was on the dun, there was a chance. That line-back dun was a cutting horse and as quick on his feet as a cat.

If any horse alive could get out of the way of that stampede, it would be the dun.

For an hour he rode back and forth across the grassy plain where the herd had been when the buffalo came. He found the remnants of a body churned into earth, but there was no way of telling who it had been.

By nightfall, working farther and farther to the west and south, they had rounded up nearly five hundred head, among them the old brindle steer who had been the leader of the herd.

"One more day," he said by the fire that night. "Just one more day, and then we leave. We've no more time."

"I wonder," the Ox said, "what become of the Indians? The ones who were, as Tell put it, ridin' in our shadow?"

Orrin reached for the coffee pot and filled his cup, then several others. He put the pot down and looked across the fire at the Ox. "Something new has been added," he said pleasantly. "What Indians?"

The Ox explained. "Tell, he left meat for them a time or two. I never saw them myself. I don't reckon he did, either."

"That dead man?" Shorty asked. "Could he have been an Indian?"

"No, he was a white man. He was wearing boots. We found the heels."

It had to be one of them. Which one?

Chapter XIV

Orrin Sackett was a careful man. He knew what he had to do, and he wanted to be about it, although, even more, he wanted to hunt for his brothers. Yet whatever else he was, he was a Sackett, and the Sacketts finished the jobs they started. Also, Tyrel and Tell, if alive, would know what he was doing and where he would be.

It was that certainty of each other that had helped them through many difficulties. They had set out to deliver cattle, and he would persist in the delivery. If Tyrel and Tell could, they would follow on and join up, and they might even be on ahead somewhere, waiting.

The situation was puzzling. The Ox was here, and they had seen what were the remains of at least one other man. According to the Ox, there had been seven, including the Chinese cook, so where were the other five?

One man could disappear easily, two almost as easily, but five, widely scattered men?

He turned his horse and rode back to the carts. The Ox rode alongside, saying nothing.

The country around was pretty wide open, and scanning it as they rode, he could see herds of antelope, most of them a mile or more away, and a good many buffalo, moving as they usually did in small herds that made up the larger group, feeding as they moved.

He could see nothing else. The antelope and buffalo

moved as if no man was near them, and he was sure there was no one out there.

The mountains, if such they could be called, had to be the answer. Before they left the country, he was going to make one sweep through those hills. He knew he could see little in that time, but there was a chance, particularly if he brought an extra man or two.

Baptiste was with the carts when they rode up, his rifle at hand. Nearby, the cattle were gathered, grazing peacefully, seemingly glad to be back together again. Across the herd he could see Charlie Fleming coming in with a small bunch of cattle. Highpockets and Shorty were at the carts, both hunkered down by the fire with cups of coffee in their hands.

Haney looked up as Orrin swung down. "We've about cleaned her up," he said, "unless you're of a mind to take the carts south, set up a new camp, and round up what went on south.

"I saw cow tracks down thataway, so we know some went on south with the buffalo." He paused. "Odd thing. Shorty an' me, we come down into a low place over yonder, and we came up on about three hundred head, all bunched and pretty, all wearin' the Sackett road brand."

Orrin was filling his cup. He sipped his coffee. "See any tracks?"

"Uh-huh. Two riders, one of them carryin' mighty light. Fresh tracks, Mr. Sackett, like those cattle had been bunched within the last few hours."

"Nobody around?"

"Nobody. It doesn't make sense. A body would think they had been bunched a-purpose and just left for us."

"No use looking gift horses in the teeth. You brought them in?"

"You're durned right! The way I figure it, we've got a shade over nine hundred head."

"Good enough. We'll move out for the northwest

tomorrow. We've lost a couple of hundred head, but we will just have to take the loss and run."

"You aimin' to look for Tell an' them?"

"Something's wrong, Haney. Five, six men missing with no sign, but somebody bunched those cows for us.

"Yes," he added, "you and me are going to take a ride into the Turtles. We couldn't cover the place in a month or more, but we can scout for tracks. If we see anything, we'll check it out. Otherwise, we'll get on with the job."

Fleming left the herd, bunching them a bit more as he circled back to the fire. He stepped down from the saddle.

"See any tracks?"

He shook his head. "Nothing, and cows are scarce, mighty scarce."

"We pull out tomorrow," Shorty said.

Fleming went to the fire, squatted on his heels, and held his cup, staring into the fire for a long minute. Then he filled his cup, avoiding the eyes of the Ox, who was staring at him.

"Good bunch of cattle," Fleming commented. "Makes a man want to get into the cow business."

Orrin threw the dregs on the ground. "Fleming, you come with Haney and me. Shorty, you stay close to the wagons with Baptiste unless you see some of the stock straying too far. But keep a rifle handy."

Orrin led the way up a dim trail into the trees. Here and there were dense stands of forest, then scatterd trees and meadows with frequent small lakes and pools. They scattered out, keeping within sight of one another but watching for tracks.

"Mr. Sackett?" Haney called out.

Orrin turned his horse and cantered over to where the tall man waited. Haney indicated the grass at his feet.

There was a place by a rotting log where a part of the grass was pressed down, and there were flecks of what appeared to be blood on the grass and the leaves. "Looks like somebody has been lyin' here, maybe a few days back."

"Horse tracks?"

"Don't see none. I reckon he was afoot. My guess would be he was bad hurt. He got this far an' just collapsed."

"Then what?"

"Well, there's a track." He pointed to their north. "I figure he came out of it and started on."

Leading their horses, they followed the tracks. Charlie Fleming was some distance away, and Orrin stood for a moment, watching him. He seemed to be studying the ground as he moved.

"Haney," Orrin said, "walk careful. If this is some of our boys, and they're hurt, they'll be wary of trouble."

"I soldiered with Tell, remember? He never shot at anything he couldn't see. He wasn't one of those damned fools who heard a noise and just blasted away."

The trail was dim and old. Whoever the wounded man was, he made over two hundred yards before he fell. They found the place where he went to his knees, then had fallen forward on his face. There had been a struggle to rise; then the fallen man had subsided and lay still for some time.

However, they found no blood on the grass. Orrin looked carefully around, searching the brush, the trees, and the grass for some indication of movement. He saw none. He looked around for Charlie Fleming, but the rider was nowhere in sight.

He moved on, taking his time, missing nothing. The wounded man had gotten back to his feet and was moving at a somewhat better pace.

"He's feelin' some better," Haney suggested.

"Either that or he suspects he's being followed and wants to hide," Orrin said.

He paused again, looking carefully around. Suddenly, he grunted and ran rapidly forward, stopping at a small cairn of three stones. Gently, he lifted off the first one, then the second.

There, placed neatly across the face of the second stone, were three parallel blades of grass.

"It's Tyrel," Orrin said.

Haney looked at the small pile of scarcely noticeable rocks. "I don't see how—!"

Orrin held up the three blades of grass. "He is the third son of my father. If there had been but one blade of grass, it would have been Tell."

"And two?"

"Me," Orrin said. "We started it when we were youngsters, playing and hunting in the woods. Tell began it when he was about nine so we boys could follow him in the woods and also so we could find our way back. Most of us have some such system, and it saves a lot of time and trouble."

"Don't tell you where he is, though."

"It will if he doesn't pass out."

"What if nobody ever comes along?"

Orrin merely glanced at him. "A Sackett always knows one of us will be along. He knows that sooner or later a Sackett will find the trail, and if at the end of it he finds a dead man, there will be some indication of who was responsible."

Haney swore softly. "I'll be damned!"

"No, but the man responsible will."

"How long's this been going on?"

"One way or another, for more than two hundred years. Oh, here and there somebody fails, but that's rare. Mostly they come through. Mostly they stick to the family tradition of helping one another.

"Tell started this system, but he had heard of it from pa. That is, he heard of something like it. This was his own idea. It doesn't have to be rocks and grass, it can be twigs, knots tied in grass, leaves, scratches on tree bark—ah!" He pointed.

At the side of a fallen branch was a sharp, triangular piece of slate, pointing off to the northwest.

"Could be an accident," Haney said skeptically.

"It could be. If so, we'll have to come back to this point and start over."

They hurried on, walking faster now. Haney was also alert, watching. It was he who saw the next mark, faint though it was. Simply three scratches on the bark of a tree.

Haney stopped. "Say! Where's Fleming?"

"He went off to the west. We'll find him later."

"I don't trust him too much," Haney said.

"Neither do I."

Orrin stopped abruptly. The tracks of three horsemen came down from the east and crossed the trail of Tyrel Sackett. Three hard-ridden horses, all shod.

"Be careful!" Haney lifted his rifle. "Those tracks are fresh!"

They faded into the brush, took the time to look around carefully, then followed the trail they had found.

Orrin stopped suddenly, studying the terrain ahead. The way seemed to lead along the side of a low hill that sloped down to a lake with a sandy shore. On the side of the hill were several clusters of trees. One of the clusters, a little higher and farther back, grew up among some rocks. There was a clump of brush and smaller trees, then two tall ones joined by a third somewhat smaller but close to the other two.

"We've found him," Orrin said.

Haney just looked, and they rode on, scrambling their horses up the bank to the clump of trees and brush.

They found him there, sprawled on fallen leaves, one hand still clutching a stick he had used to help him along. There was blood on the top of his shoulder near his neck where a bullet had cut through the muscle, and his right leg was swollen to almost twice its normal size. He had split the pants leg to ease the binding effect on the swollen leg, which showed black and blue through the gaping hole.

"Haney," Orrin said, "you ride back to the carts and get a spare horse. Keep your eyes open for Fleming on the way back, and tell the boys to sit tight and guard the cattle. I won't try to move him tonight. Bring the horse up in the morning."

When Haney had ridden off, Orrin cleared a place of leaves, scraping them well back, and then he put together a small fire of twigs and bits of bark. The flame was too small and too well hidden by the trunks of the trees and the brush to be seen. As for the smoke, it would be dissipated by rising through the foliage of the trees until spread so thin as to be invisible.

He made a bed of piled leaves, and with water from his canteen he bathed the wound. It was going to be troublesome but not dangerous, and from past experience he knew the dangers of infection were few in the fresh pure air of the western country.

When he had made Tyrel comfortable, he led his horse to water at the lake, then let him graze on a small patch of grass not far from the cluster of trees where he could watch both the horse and Tyrel. When it started to become dark, he led the horse into the brush, which was some protection from the mosquitoes, and settled down beside his small fire.

It was then he thought to check Tyrel's six-shooter. Four chambers had been fired; two remained loaded. He reloaded the empty chambers and thrust the gun back into its holster.

He might have been shooting to try to turn the stampede; if not, somebody was dead.

Darkness made a mystery of the forest and goblins of the trees.

He added a knot to the coals and dozed with arabesques of shadow-play upon his dark, hawklike features.

A whisper of sound, the faint crunching of a branch,

and his eyes opened wide, and his gun slid into his hand. Something black and ominous loomed in the open space between two trees. His gun was up, his thumb ready on the hammer.

It was Tyrel's line-back dun.

Chapter XV

Highpockets Haney reached the group of trees before the first light, but Orrin already had Tyrel on the dun.

"See anybody?"

"Not a soul." He paused. "Fleming was in camp, wondering what had become of us. He brought in two, three head of young stuff he found in the brush."

"No sign of anybody else?"

"He says he saw nothing."

Tyrel was obviously suffering from a mild concussion, and when he became conscious, he showed no disposition to talk. When asked about Tell, he merely shrugged. The stampede had caught them scattered about the herd, and they had remained scattered.

Orrin rode ahead, scouting for trouble. He had a feeling they'd find it before the day was over.

"Shorty's starting the herd," Haney said. "Baptiste and his carts will bring up the drag. We should see them when we come out of the trees." They were skirting a small pond, and Tyrel's horse took a sudden turn, and he groaned.

"He's got a bad leg there," Orrin said. "It doesn't seem to be broken but bruised like you wouldn't believe. Horse must have fallen or something of the kind."

They sighted the herd as they came into the open. Shorty had them moving; Fleming was on the far side with the carts bringing up the rear. Baptiste stopped when he saw them, and with great care they loaded Tyrel into one of the carts, making a place for him among the sacks, his rifle beside him. They tied the dun behind the cart in which he was riding.

Haney fell into place with the herd, and Orrin stayed off to one side, watching the country around for some movement or sign of life. He saw nothing.

Somewhere out there was Tell or what was left of him. Somewhere were other hands, lost in the same stampede. The Ox he could see working alongside the herd, but what had become of *his* partner? The man Orrin had not yet seen?

Uneasily, Orrin rubbed the stubble of beard on his chin. Shaving every day had become a habit, and he had a dislike of going unshaven no matter where he was.

He was reluctant to leave the area without finding Tell, but Tell, had he been present, would have insisted they get on with the job. Wherever he was, if he was alive, Tell was doing what was needful.

Tyrel was sleeping when he rode by the carts, so there was no chance to try to learn more from him even if he knew more, which was doubtful.

Wide rolled the prairies before their roving eyes, and steadily the cattle moved on, pointing the way to the northwest. All day they walked, and the day following and the next. Somewhere, Orrin supposed, they had reached or would reach the border and pass into Canada. There was no marker, and he looked for none.

They camped by small creeks, near a slough, or in some small meadow where the cattle could feed. They saw no Indians and no wildlife but flocks of antelope, always within view, or buffalo. Prairie wolves hung on their flanks, watching for the animal who might trail too far behind.

Ten miles that first day because of the late start, fifteen and sixteen on the days following. On the third day, Tyrel spent part of the day in the saddle. At night, they sat beside the campfire.

"They came right out of the prairie," he explained. "Suddenly, we heard the thunder of hoofs, and they came over the rise like a black thunder cloud.

"We were all scattered out; there was no chance or time to do anything but try to get out of the way, and that's just what we did. The cattle turned ahead of that herd and began to run with them. There was nothing anybody could do, and even the cattle had no choice but to run. Otherwise, they'd have been trampled into the ground. I heard a scream, but, Orrin, I doubt if it was one of our boys. I don't recall anybody being where that scream came from."

"We found some remains, but they were so trampled we could only tell it had been a man and more than likely a white man."

"I doubt if he was one of ours. Brandy was within sight when the buffalo came into sight, and I had time to wave him out of there. Lin—he was our Chinese cook—he was out behind the herd somewhere, and I think it missed him altogether."

"Who shot you?"

"That happened later. There were three of them, and they were hunting me, or maybe just any survivors.

"A big buffalo bull tossed the dun and me, and when we went down, he came in with his head down to gore us. He hooked, but his horn hit my saddle and so saved the dun. Then I struck my six-shooter in his ear and squeezed her off.

"That bull just naturally rolled over, and the dun scrambled up, and I started to. Seemed that buffalo bull rammed his head into my leg just about the time I was sticking my gun barrel in his ear.

"I got the dun over to me and grabbed a stirrup and pulled myself up. By that time my leg was hurting.

"Well, I taken a look around. The cattle were scattered to kingdom come, and there was nobody in sight but some buzzards."

Tyrel refilled his cup. "Being one who is apt to accept the situation and take it from there, I considered.

"Here I was out in the middle of nowhere and maybe the only one left alive. You were on a steamboat or maybe in a cart coming west. I had me a good horse, although he was some irritated at being knocked over, and I had fifteen hundred pounds of buffalo meat, hide, and bone.

"So I gathered me some buffalo chips and put together a fire. Then I cut out some buffalo steak and broiled about four or five pounds of it. When that was done, I cut myself some more meat, tied it up in some buffalo hide, and climbed into the saddle.

"It was when I tried to get into the saddle that I realized I was in trouble. It durned near killed me."

"You ain't told me about those empty chambers."

"Comin' to it. I'd ridden a far piece, but my leg was givin' me what for, and I rode in under the trees, grabbed hold of a limb, and pulled myself up from the saddle and then kind of lowered myself down to the ground.

"Next thing I knew, they come up on me. I was backed up to a tree, and the dun had walked off, grazin', and there was three of them. Right away I spotted them for what they were. They were goin' to kill me, all right, but first they were going to tell me how awful mean and tough they were.

"You know the kind. We've met them before. They were talkers. They just had to run off at the mouth awhile before they did anything.

"There were three of them, and they didn't know me from Adam's off-ox. They knew I had been with the cattle and contrary to what we'd figured, it had been them who started the stampede and not the Sioux.

"They started tellin' me about it. And they started to tell me what they were going to do.

"Me, I listened to them a mite, and then I said, 'What did you fellows come up here for?'

"'We're goin' to kill you!' This big redhead was saying that, with a nasty grin on his face.

"'So you're going to kill me? Then what the hell is all the talk for?'

"That kind of took the wind out of them, and as I spoke, I just fetched my piece.

116

"Didn't seem to me like they'd ever seen a fast draw before. Two of them went down, and the third one taken off, or maybe his horse ran off with him. Anyway, you couldn't see him for dust."

"And you saw nothing of Tell?"

Tyrel shook his head. He was obviously tired, and Orrin asked no more questions. The night was quiet, and the herd had bedded down.

Baptiste had added to his duties the care of Tyrel's injured leg. The flesh wound gave no particular trouble, and with Baptiste caring for it, the swelling in the leg reduced slowly.

Orrin forded the cattle across the Mouse and pointed the herd toward Pipestone Creek, some distance off to the northwest by the route they were following.

"We've got to figure it this way," Orrin said over a campfire. "The stampede was not caused by Indians but apparently by white men.

"Now who would want to do such a thing? Thieves who wished to steal our cattle? Maybe. Some of the 'Higginses' Logan spoke about? That's more likely.

"Somebody, for some reason we do not know, wishes to prevent our cattle from reaching their destination. So far they've done us some damage, but they haven't stopped us, so it's likely they will try again.

"From what Tyrel says, at least two of them won't be showing up again. That may make them back off completely, but we can't depend on that. We will have to take it for granted they will come again, and soon.

"We've got some extra rifles. I want them loaded and ready, and every camp must be a fort."

Orrin glanced over at the Ox, who was simply listening and offering no comment or even an acknowledgement that he heard.

Yet, in the days that followed, all their preparations seemed for nothing. The mornings came one after another, each crisp and clear, and the days warmed. The grass was green on all the hills now. There were several light showers and a thunderstorm that brought a crashing downpour that lasted for less than an hour.

The Qu'Appelle River lay somewhere before them and off to the west the Moose Mountains.

Orrin found himself thinking of Nettie. She should be well on her way to Fort Carlton now, far away to the north. He would probably not see her again. The thought made him melancholy, yet there was nothing to be done. Their way lay west, and if Tell were alive, he would be coming on to join them if by some chance he was not already there before them.

Occasionally, they saw the bones of buffalo, once the antlers of a deer. Occasionally, there were other bones, unfamiliar to a quick glance, but there was no time to pause and examine them. They pushed on, accompanied by the creaking, groaning wheels of the Red River carts.

Tyrel's bruised leg remained sore and stiff, but his flesh wound healed rapidly, as wounds usually did on the plains and in the mountains. He took to riding a little more each day, usually scouting wide of the drive and only returning to it occasionally.

"Something's not right," he commented once. "I can smell trouble."

"The Ox is worried," Orrin added. "He's got something on his mind. That partner of his, I guess. Gilcrist, his name was. Or so he said."

"Good a name as any," Tyrel said. "Out here, if a man doesn't like his name, he can choose his own, and a lot of folks have."

"He never talks to Fleming," Orrin said. "At least, I haven't seen them even near one another for days."

A brief but violent thunderstorm came with the afternoon. Fort Qu'Appelle was nearby, but there was no need to stop, and when the storm passed, he led the drive on past the fort. However, he had gone but a mile or less when a party of riders appeared. Several Indians, Crees by the look of them, rode up. While the cattle moved on, Orrin waited with Baptiste and the carts.

The Indians were friendly, curious as to where the

cattle were being taken and about the Sioux, with whom they were only occasionally friendly.

Tyrel rode to meet them when they finally caught up.

"Picked up some sign," he said. "Something you should see, Orrin."

"Trouble?"

"Maybe."

Orrin glanced at the sun. "We've got a few miles of driving ahead of us. All right, let's go look!"

The tracks were two miles ahead of the herd. At least five riders had come up from the southwest and had met a half-dozen riders coming down from the northeast. They had dismounted, built a small fire, and made coffee. The coffee grounds had been thrown out when they emptied their pot for packing.

"Maybe a dozen men riding well-shod horses," Tyrel said, "and they rode off to the west together."

Orrin nodded. He had been poking around the campfire and looking at tracks.

"Just for luck, Tye," he said, "let's turn due north for a spell."

"Toward Fort Carlton?" Tyrel asked, his eyes too innocent.

Orrin flushed. "Well, it seems a good idea."

Chapter XVI

When first it come to me that I was alive, I was moving. For what seemed a long time, I lay there with my eyes closed and just feeling the comfort of lying still. Then I tried to move, and everything hurt, and I mean everything.

Then I got to wondering where I was and what was moving me and what was I doing flat on my back when there was work to be done?

When I tried to move my right arm, I could, and my hand felt for my gun, and it was gone. So was my gun belt and holster. Yet I wasn't tied down, so it must be that I was with friendly folks. About that time, I realized I was riding on a travois pulled behind an Indian pony.

After a bit, I closed my eyes and must have passed out again because the next thing I knew we were standing still. I was lying flat out on the ground, and I could hear a fire crackling and smell meat broiling.

Now when a body has been around as long as me, he collects a memory for smells, and the smells told me even without opening my eyes that I was in an Indian camp.

About that time, an Indian came over to me, and he saw my eyes were open, and he said something in an Indian dialect I hadn't heard before, and an Indian woman came over to look at me. I tried to sit up, and although it hurt like hell, I managed it. Didn't seem I had any broken bones, but I was likely bruised head to foot, which can be even more painful sometimes.

She brought me a bowl with some broth in it, and

whatever else was wrong with me hadn't hurt my appetite. The man who had found me awake was a young man, strongly made but limping.

A youngster, walking about, came over and stared at me with big round eyes, and I smiled at him. When I had put away two bowls of broth, an old Indian came to me with my gun belt and holster. My six-shooter was in it, and he handed it to me. First thing, I checked the loads, and they were there.

The old man squatted beside me. "Much cows, all gone," he said. He gestured to show they'd scattered every which way.

"Men?" I asked.

He shrugged and pointed across the way, and I saw another man lying on the ground a dozen feet away. I raised up a bit and looked. It was Lin, the Chinese cook.

"How bad?"

"Much bad. Much hurt." He looked over at Lin and then said, "White man?"

"Chinese," I said.

The word meant nothing to him, so I drew a diagram in the dust, showing where we now were, the south Saskatchewan and the mountains of British Columbia. That he grasped quickly. Then I made a space and said, "Much water." Beyond it, I drew a coast and indicated China. "His home," I said.

He studied it, then indicated British Columbia and drew his eyes thin to seem like Lin's. "Indian," he said, "here."

It was true. A long time since I had been told by a man in the Sixth Cavalry that some of the Indians from the northwest coast had eyes like the Chinese.

After a while, I went to sleep and was only awakened when they were ready to offer me food; it was daybreak.

The young Indian who had been wounded and on the travois when first we encountered them carried a rifle of British make. The older men were armed only with bows. We were heading northwest, but I asked no

121

questions, being content to just lie and rest. What had happened to me, I did not know, but I suspected a mild concussion and that I had fallen and been dragged. My shoulders were raw, I discovered, and had been treated with some herbs by a squaw.

On the following day, I got up and could move around. Then one old Indian, who seemed to be in authority if anyone was, showed me my saddle, bridle, saddlebags, and rifle, carefully cared for on another travois. I left the riding gear where it was but took up the rifle, at which the old man showed approval. Seemed to me they expected grief and were glad to have another fighting man on his feet.

Lin had a broken leg. He was skinned up and bruised not unlike what happened to me, but he had the busted leg to boot. They'd set the bone, put splints on the leg, and bound it up with wet rawhide, which had dried and shrunk tight around the leg.

"Where are the others?"

I walked beside him as we moved. "No tellin'. Dead, maybe. Scattered to the winds, maybe. All you've got to do is get well."

Well, I was a long way from being a well man. Before the day was over, I was so tired I could scarce drag. They made camp in a tree-lined hollow with a small waterhole and a bunch of poplars.

We'd lost all track of time, Lin an' me. We'd both been unconscious, and we didn't know how long. I'd no idea what had become of my horse or the remuda stock we had, and we'd lost all our cattle.

Only thing I could say for us was that we were headin' in the right direction and we were alive.

What I needed was a horse. This was the first time I'd been caught afoot in a long time, and I didn't like it. I should be scouting the country, hunting for Tyrel and roundin' up cows.

Lin was feeling better. As for me, I limped along with a head aching something fierce and a disposition that would frighten a grizzly. Not that I let those Indian folks see it, but, believe me, I was sore.

Meanwhile, a way out in the western mountains, Logan was in trouble and wishful of our coming.

As to Tyrel, he might be killed dead, but I misdoubted that. Tyrel was just too downright ornery to be killed that easy. If he ever went down to death, there'd be bodies stacked all about, you could bet on that.

One thing about a Sackett, he finishes what he starts if it is a good thing to start. All of us knew that whatever else was happening, we'd be pushing on west. West was where I was going, and if I arrived there with no cows, I'd round up a buffalo herd and drive it in, or try.

If that failed, I'd have to get a rattlesnake for a whip and drive a flock of grizzlies. Right now I was mad enough to do it.

It so happened that at the time of the stampede these Indians were a way off to one side where they'd had to go to camp on water. The stampede went right by, an easy half mile off.

"Where do you go?" I asked the old man.

He gestured to the northwest. They were going back to some place; that was all I could gather. His English was limited, and I spoke none of the Indian tongues that made sense to him. It was a rare thing to find an Indian who spoke any language but his own, although some had picked up some French or English because of trade.

Their direction was our direction, so we stayed with them. Besides, they needed us. The young warrior was still not able to travel far when hunting, and neither of the old men had much luck with hunting. Their food was mostly small game or roots picked hither and yon.

The meat I'd left them had been a godsend.

Soon as I was fit, I scouted around some of an evening. First evening I had no luck; never even saw anything worth shooting until the second day when I spotted a buffalo calf.

It was a week before Lin could walk, even a little, and by that time we'd traveled most of a hundred miles. It was that night by the fire that Little Bear came to me. He was the youngster walking about, and me and him had talked a good deal, neither understanding too much except that we liked one another.

He had been out setting snares, and he came to me by the fire. "A horse!" he said.

"That's it, son. That's what I need."

He pointed off to the east. "A horse!" he repeated.

"You mean you've seen a horse?"

When he said yes, I went to my saddle and took my rope from it. "You show me," I said.

Our horses had been scattered when the stampede took place, and it might just be one of our own. Not that it would be any easier to catch.

We walked maybe a mile, and he pointed. Sure enough, feeding along the shadow of some poplars was a dun horse.

Now Tyrel and me, we both rode line-back duns, probably get of the same sire, as we'd caught them out of a wild bunch who ran with a powerful old dun stallion. The stallion was no horse to catch. He'd run wild too long; he was too strong and too mean. A horse like that will never stop fighting, and he'll either kill somebody or himself.

At that distance, I couldn't make out whether that was Tyrel's dun or mine. But he'd been riding his when the stampede hit us, so this one must be mine. There was a shadow from the trees, or I might have guessed which one it was.

Anyway, we moved toward him.

His head came up sharp, and he looked at me with ears pricked and he let me come on.

When I was within fifty yards, he shied away a mite, but he didn't run, and I called to him. He walked toward me then, and I rubbed his neck a little, and he seemed glad to be back with folks again. I rigged a hackamore and led him back to camp. Next morning, when we started out, I was in the saddle and felt like a whole man again.

The wind began to pick up, the grass bending before it, and I was scouting ahead looking for game when I came on some tracks.

Little Bear looked at them and pointed toward the direction they'd taken. "You cattle," he said. "Two mans!"

Maybe thirty head of cattle and two riders, and we set off after them.

We found them bedded down near a slough alongside a capful of fire with some meat broiling.

" 'Light an' set!" Cap said, like he'd seen me only that morning. "Brandy an' me got a few of your cows."

It was good to see them. They had six horses, two of them strange, wearing a Lazy Y brand.

"You don't look the worse for wear," I said.

"Pure-dee luck! We was out in front, and we run for it. We had fast horses, an' after a mile or two, we managed to cut away to the side. Seen anybody else?"

"Lin's alive. He's with the Indians."

Little Bear rode off to get his people, and we set by the fire explainin' to each other what happened.

"All we can do," I said, "is head north to meet Orrin. He'll have grub, and if there's anybody else alive, they'll come to that rendezvous."

"That's how I figured it." Cap glanced over at me. "You see the tracks? It wasn't Sioux."

"We know."

"I wonder what Logan's tied into, anyway?"

The smell of the wood fire was almighty nice, and I felt right just having a horse again. I've spent so much time sittin' on the hurricane deck of a horse that I ain't at home anywhere else.

Little Bear's folks came in shy of midnight, and we all bedded down close together, with Cap, Brandy, an' me sharin' time with the cows.

Cap an' Brandy were sure enough hungry. They'd been eatin' squirrel, rabbit, and skunk most of the time since the stampede, when they ate anything at all.

"There's hills up ahead," Cap said. "Maybe we'll

run into Orrin an' his carts. Those are the Thunder Breeding Hills. If he didn't find anything west of the Turtles, he'd keep on west, wouldn't he?"

"He would. Or I think he would."

Yet I was worried. We were a long way from the mines, we had only thirty head or so, we were short on riding stock, and we had no grub or ammunition. We'd lost the biggest part of our outfit, and we were riding strange country.

There were Sioux around, and there were the white renegades who'd attacked before. Yet it felt good to be back with Cap. Brandy and Lin were new men, but Cap I knew from way back. Any kind of a stir-up, be it work or fight, Cap would stand his ground.

The cattle had lost weight. A stampede can run a good many pounds off a critter, and these had been driven hard since.

The way we drove them was across a prairie with islands of brush and occasional swamps. Time or two we had to stop and rope some old mossyhorn out of the bog. Those islands of brush worried me because a body could get close to a man before he realized. And they did.

All of a sudden, Cap ups with his hand and outs with his Winchester, and we saw three men ride into view from behind a clump of brush.

I had no idea who they were but had a mighty good idea they weren't friendly.

Chapter XVII

The sun lay bright upon the land ahead and bright upon the three horsemen who rode to meet us.

Cap glanced around. "Good boy," he said. "Brandy's facin' the other way. So's Lin."

The Indians were behind us and to the right, concealed from the riders by the brush.

"There will be more of them," Cap said.

"There will," I agreed, and glanced at the small lake that lay ahead and to the right. It was likely they would attack from the left and try to drive us toward the lake. The three riders were too obvious.

"Howdy, boys! Huntin' for something?"

"Lookin' to buy cattle." The speaker was a big, bearded man in a buckskin coat worked with blue and red beads. He had a rifle in his hand and a fur cap.

"Sorry. These are not for sale."

"Make you a good offer?" His horse was sidling around, and I saw him throw a quick glance toward left rear.

"Not for sale, boys," I said. I rode out from the herd a little and toward the right, outflanking them a little, and I could see they didn't like it.

Cap had promptly shifted a little to the left, and I said, "Better move, boys. We're coming through!"

"Sell 'em," the big man repeated, "or we'll take them!"

"All right, *Brandy!*" I yelled, and he let out a whoop and started the cattle.

They were headed that way, and cattle like to go where they're pointed, so they started moving. Brandy let out another whoop, and one of the steers turned right at the nearest horsemen.

The sudden rush of cattle split the three riders. Two went one way and one the other, and the nearest one was coming my way, so I headed right at him. In trying to swing wide of a head-on collision, he put his horse into the soft ground at the lake's edge, and his horse floundered in the mud, his rider swearing.

Wheeling the dun, I raced along the flank of the moving cattle, heard two quick shots from behind, and saw Lin on the ground, his horse beside him; he was shooting across a fallen log.

A half-dozen riders had come from behind one of those clumps of brush, and Lin, being on the ground, had the advantage.

I saw a horse stumble and go down, pitching his rider over his head. Mud leaped in front of another rider, and his horse swerved sharply, and a third bullet had him dropping his rifle and grabbing for a mane hold as his horse went charging away, cutting across the front of the other riders.

It all happened in seconds. Two men were down, a horse running wild and the cattle charging. The big man with the beard threw up his rifle to shoot at me, but Cap burned him with a quick shot, and my bullet burned his hand. What other damage it did, I couldn't see, but I did see a splash of blood on the buckskin coat and on the saddle.

Lin was back in the saddle and riding up the flank of the small herd, and we swung the cattle past the lake and into the open toward some sand hills looming ahead.

Brandy closed in behind the herd, and we moved them out of there.

Cap Rountree closed in toward me. "Pilgrims," he said contemptuously. "They haven't burned the powder we have."

"We were lucky. Next time, we may not get the breaks."

We pushed the cattle on, keeping a lookout on all

sides. What Cap said was obviously true. The men who had attacked us were tough men and hard but not seasoned fighting men.

Any man can take a gun in hand and go out to use it, and often enough he is braver because of that gun. But fighting is like playing poker. You have to pay to learn, and you only learn with the cards in hand and money on the table. Cap and me, well, we had been through more fights in any one year of our lives than most men get in a lifetime.

Me? Well, I'd been fightin' one way or another all my life. Cap had begun as a mountain man, and he'd fought Sioux, Cheyenne, Blackfeet, Comanches, Kiowas, and Apaches, and he still had his hair.

"That youngster," Cap said, "he'll do to take along. He was almighty cool."

"So was Lin," I added. "Don't discount that heathen Chinee."

"Heathen? Hell!" Cap spat. "He knows more than both of us. Why we was talkin' the other night, and he come up with some of the damndest stuff you ever heard!"

We were not through with fighting, and we knew it, so we moved the cattle along faster than we should have to keep the weight on them. We wanted to get to some place where we could make a stand. We'd got by them, but they still outnumbered us, and we could expect trouble.

"Maybe we should take it to them," Cap suggested. "Discourage them. I'm a pretty good horse thief when need be."

"Good idea," I suggested, "but let's try for distance."

"How you fixed for ca'tridges?"

"Short," I said. "We've got to avoid a fight if we can."

"Wished Orrin would show up."

"Or Tyrel and the boys with those packhorses. We're going to need them, Cap. Need them bad."

Spotting a long, sandy draw, I turned the herd down

it, as the sand was deep and left few tracks. There was small hope that it would help, but we needed every advantage.

Toward nightfall, we turned up another draw, crossed a gravely hill, and camped on a knoll close to a small grove. We built our fire for coffee inside the grove where the glow of the fire was hidden. The cattle, exhausted from the drive, grazed only a little before lying down.

"One man on guard," I said. "We all need rest. Stay on the ground and don't skyline yourself."

After they were settled and we had eaten, I walked out from the camp. Nothing could be seen but the darkness of the trees and brush. The cattle merged with the darkness.

While the others slept, I took count as well as I could without disturbing them. I could see fourteen cartridges in Cap's belt, eight in Brandy's. Lin had no belt but might have some in his pockets. How many were in their rifles I could not guess. My rifle was fully loaded as was my six-shooter. Nine bullets remained in my belt. We'd be lucky to survive any kind of an Indian fight or any other.

Shortly before daybreak, we drove off the hill, found a small stream, and walked the cattle in the water for over a mile. That such tactics would delay them more than a little was unlikely, yet at least some of the attackers had been greenhorns.

Who, then, were they? There had been no attempt of which I knew to steal our cattle. They seemed more interested in stopping or delaying us.

Leaving the water, we found where a herd of buffalo had passed and followed in their tracks, losing our trail in theirs.

We watered that night in the Qu'Appelle River. It had been named, so we heard, because an Indian, dropping down the river in a canoe, thought he heard a call from the bank. He waited, listening, then called out himself. There was no reply, so he went on, but since then it has been the Who Calls River. At least that was the story Kootenai Brown told me one night by the fire.

Cap and me looked for cart tracks but found none. There could be other carts, of course, but we knew ours had not passed.

We crossed the river where there were no bluffs and bedded our few cattle on the far bank. It was not a good place, and Cap grumbled a good bit.

Wolves prowled close around the camp, and we did not wish to attract attention by firing a shot. Several times, we took flaming sticks from the fire and charged at them, but they soon came back.

Between mosquitoes, sand flies, and wolves, we had little sleep. When morning came, I was up early and in a bad mood. There was little to eat, and nobody talked much.

There was crisp grass and sand with occasional swamps. Several times steers went into the swamps to escape the flies, and we had to throw a loop around their horns and drag them out. It made nobody any happier. By the time nightfall arrived, I was almost hoping for a fight, being that irritable.

Yet it was pretty country. There were bluebells and wild roses everywhere and a few small tiger lilies growing here and there. At one place, we came upon acres of bluebells.

In camp, Brandy sat opposite me nursing a cup of coffee, one of the last we'd have if Orrin didn't find us.

"What month is it?" Brandy said. "I lost track of the days. Now I'm not even sure of the month."

"June," I replied, and the thought made me no happier. Time was a getting on, and we'd a far piece to go before snow fell, and at the end we had to find our way through mountains we didn't know and where trails were, we had heard, mighty few.

Looking at the cattle gave me no pleasure. They'd started out in fine shape, but due to long drives and the necessity to keep moving, they'd lost weight.

We had seen no buffalo or even an antelope for days. "We can always kill a beef," Cap suggested.

131

"We may have to," I said.

Come to think of it, Cap was looking gaunt himself, and Brandy, too. Lin, he never seemed to change, grub or no. His leg, despite the fall, was better.

"We'll lay up tomorrow," I suggested. "Maybe we can catch us a mess of fish."

The horses, too, were in bad shape. The rest, little as it was, would do them good, and they did not have to worry about food. There was grass enough to pasture half the stock in Canada.

It was almighty hot. We let the stock feed, and we let them drink. When we moved on, there was going to be none too much water.

Cap was the fisherman amongst us. Him and Lin. Both of them caught a mess of fish, but Brandy and me couldn't catch cold.

We had fish for supper, and we had fish for breakfast, and nothing tasted any better, seasoned a mite with wild garlic.

We were riding out to start the cattle when I saw our Indian friends. One of them rode up to where we were with a chunk of fresh venison. We took a look at each other and got down from the saddle and broiled and ate it right on the spot.

Little Bear waited, and then he said, "White man comes."

"A white man? Where?"

"I see him, alone."

Something about his manner bothered me. It seemed he wanted to tell me more than he knew how, but he just said, "He ride here."

"You mean he's coming here?"

"He comes here. He rides here."

Cap got up and wiped his hands on his chaps. "I think he's tryin' to tell you this gent rides for you."

We looked back toward the river. "Let him come on," I said. "We've miles to go."

We started them out and hadn't gone fifty yards when we saw a lone buffalo calf. When he saw us, he bawled.

"Lost his ma," Cap said. "Shall we take him along?"

"Why not?"

Cap rode wide and started the calf toward the herd. He did not take to being driven, but the herd had its attractions. Finally, he galloped off and joined the cattle.

We were a good half mile into the sand hills under a blistering sun when the rider caught up with us. We heard him coming, and I turned in the saddle.

"Well," Cap said, "we can use every hand we can get."

He should have been having a hard time of it, but he didn't look like hard times. He looked fat and sassy like he'd been eating mighty well. He rode up and said, "Howdy! I've missed you boys!"

It was Gilcrist.

Chapter XVIII

"You come out alive," Gilcrist said.

"All of us," I said. "Where've you been?"

"Huntin' for you. Livin' off the country."

"Must've been good country," Cap commented.

Gilcrist turned sharply, but Cap's features were bland and innocent. Gilcrist turned back to me. "Lost some cattle, I see. Ain't much use in goin' on with this little bunch."

"Beef is beef," I said. "I never knew a mining camp to turn down good beef cattle."

He started to speak, then changed his mind. He turned his mount to ride away, and I watched him drop back to where Lin was riding.

"Notice that?" I said to Cap. "He never asked about the Ox. You'd think a man would at least want to know what happened to his partner."

"Maybe he knows," Cap commented. "Maybe he knows just a whole lot that we don't. If that man's been livin' off the country, he's the luckiest hunter I ever did see."

They rode on for a short distance, and Cap said, "He's right about the cattle, though. What are all of us doin' drivin' this little ol' bunch of cows? Even sayin' they need beef, this is a mighty small bunch."

"We taken a contract to deliver beef," I said, "and we're going to deliver beef if there's only one cow left when we get there, but I've a hunch we'll have a sight more.

"Where's Tyrel? Where's Orrin? Those boys are

somewhere, and if they're alive, they'll have some stock. I'd bet on it.

"Orrin now, he's turned lawyer, but he can still read more'n law books. He can read sign. He's comin' along a trail where he knows we're supposed to be. He's going to be lookin' for sign, and he will learn as much from what he doesn't see as what he does. If he doesn't find cattle sign where he expects to find it, he will start hunting for it.

"Orrin's a good hand on a trail, and he will know as much of what happened as if we'd left a written-out guide for him.

"What we've got to study on is what's wrong at the other end? What happened to Logan? Why can't he help himself? Who's threatening to hang him? What's he need the cattle for?"

"Seems plain enough," Cap said. "If he can't help himself, he must be sick, hurt, or in jail. Knowin' something of Logan, I'd say he's in jail. He's too mean and tough to be hurt."

"You may be right. Some of those Clinch Mountain boys are rough. Nice folks, but don't start nothing unless you want trouble."

"What's he need the cattle for?"

"God only knows! The folks up there need them for beef, that's plain enough. They've probably hunted the country until all the game's been killed off or fled, and minin' men have to eat."

"You thought about gettin' cattle in over the trails?" Cap asked. "You an' me, we've covered some rough country, but mostly we just walked or rode over it. We never tried to move no cattle along those trails.

"There's trails up yonder where if a man makes a misstep, he can fall for half a mile. Same thing goes for a cow."

We were in the sand hills now, and water was scarce. Somewhere ahead of us was the elbow of the Saskatchewan or what the Indians called "The River That Turns." The cattle began to labor to get through the sand; at times, some of them stopped, ready to give up. We found no water, and the heat was almost unbearable.

Cap came to me, mopping his brow. "We got to find water, Tell. We've got too few horses, and they're about played out. On a drive like this, we should have three or four horses per man, at least."

"I wish we had them."

All day they struggled through the sand hills, and only as dark was closing in did they find a small lake that was not brackish. Many of the cattle walked belly deep in the water to drink.

Lin had a fire going when they bunched the cattle on a nearby flat. Leaving Cap and Brandy with the cattle, I headed in for camp with Gilcrist riding along. The boys had done a great job with the cattle, and they deserved credit. Even Gilcrist had done his part, and I said so.

He glanced at me. "Didn't know you noticed."

"I don't miss much," I said. "You did your share."

"You've got some good hands."

"Cap's worth two of any of the rest of us. He's forgotten more than the rest of us will ever know."

They were pulling up at camp, and as I swung down, Gilcrist asked, "You serious about goin' all the way through?"

"Never more serious."

"You'll never make it, Sackett. Nobody's ever taken cattle into that country. Nobody can."

A moment there, I stopped, my hands on the saddle, and I looked across at him. "There's some folks who hope we won't make it, and they want to keep us from making it, but they don't know what they're up against."

"Maybe you don't."

"We had a run-in with some of that outfit. Let me tell you something, Gilcrist. If they want to stop us, they ought to stop sending a bunch of tenderfeet to do it. Just because a man can shoot, it doesn't turn him into a fightin' man. If we had started to fight back, there wouldn't be a man of that bunch alive. It scares me to think what would happen if that bunch of thugs happened to run into a war party of Blackfeet!"

Gilcrist dismounted. He started to speak, then changed his mind. Walking along, I picked up sticks for the fire, then walked around gathering what fuel I could.

Lin glanced at me when I dropped the fuel. "The Indian boy came in. He says there is somebody following us. A big outfit."

Lin was picking up the western lingo. He started slicing meat into a pan for frying, and he said, "The Indians had not seen the outfit, just heard them and seen their dust."

"Dust?"

"A lot of it."

Gilcrist came in and sat down. "You say somebody was coming?"

"Indians," I told him. "Somebody saw some Indians."

I surely wasn't lying about that. How much he'd heard, I didn't know. Soon the boys started coming in.

Gilcrist was looking across the fire at me. "I'd no idea you were the Sackett who rode with the Sixth. They used to say you were good with a gun."

"You hear all sorts of stories."

Cap spat into the fire. "Them ain't stories. You can take it from me, Gil, an' I've seen 'em all! There ain't anybody who is any better!"

Gilcrist started to speak, stopped, then said, "You ain't seen 'em all. You ain't seen me."

"I hope I never do," Cap said dryly.

Gilcrist stared at him. "I don't know how to take that."

Cap smiled. "I just hate to see a man get killed," he said. "You or anybody else."

"I ain't goin' to get killed."

Cap smiled again. "I helped bury twenty men who thought the same thing."

It was a quiet night. We ate and turned in, all of us

dog tired. The stars were out, bright as lanterns in the sky, but nobody stayed awake long. Those days, when a man works from can see to can't see, he just naturally passes out when he hits the bed. It was long days of hard work and no chance for daydreaming when the cattle were dry and wanting water.

Only Cap and me, we set late by the fire. I was thinking of what was to come. As for him, I didn't know what he was thinking about. Or didn't until he said, "You want me to ride back and see who that is? It may be trouble."

"Not you. Anybody but you. A body can always find another cowhand but a good cook? No way you can find another cook without a miracle."

There was a-plenty to consider. We were down to our last coffee, and as for other grub, we'd been making do on what we could rustle for days. Looked to me like we would have to strike north for Fort Carlton and lay in a stock of grub. It was going to throw us back, but I saw no way out of it.

Carlton was due north. Thinking of that, I wondered, but not aloud, about trying to go west from there. Traveling in strange country like this, where I knew nothing of the rivers. If there was a practical route west from Fort Carlton, we might lose no time at all.

"All right," I said to Cap, "we'll swing north."

"You want I should have a look at who that is comin' up the line?"

"I'll go."

"You're tired, man. You need rest."

"Why, you old buffalo chaser, you say I'm tired? What about you?"

"You lose me, you ain't lost much. You get lost, and we're all up the creek."

Well, I got up and roped me a horse. "Stand by for trouble, Cap," I told him. "I think we've got it coming."

With that I rode off west. It was dark when I

started, but that was a good night horse I had between my knees, and we found a trail that left the creek and went up on the bluffs. Off to the east, I spotted a campfire.

Down a trail through the forest, winding down where darkness was, winding among the silent trees. Only the hoof falls of my horse, only the soft whispering of night creatures moving. Now I was riding where danger might be. I was riding where a man's life might hang in the wind, ready to be blown away by the slightest chance, yet I will not lie and say I did not like it.

That horse was easy in the night, moving like a cat on dainty feet. He knew we were riding into something, he knew there might be the smell of gunpowder, but he liked it, too. You could sense it in the way he moved. A man riding the same horse a lot comes to know his feelings and ways, for no two are alike, and I was one to make companions of my horses, and they seemed to understand. They knew we were in this together.

Time and again, I drew up to listen. A man can't ride careless into wild country. The banks of the river had an easier slope below the elbow, and some grassy tongues of land pushed into the river. There was a rustling of water along the banks and a dampness in the air near the river. My horse pricked his ears, and we walked slowly forward. I heard no unnatural sound, smelled nothing until I caught a faint smell of wood smoke, and then a moment later an animal smell.

Cattle! I drew up again. There was much brush, almost as high as my head, but scattered. Suddenly, sensing something near, I drew rein again.

There were cattle near, and a large herd. I could smell them and hear the faint sounds a herd will make at night, the soft moanings, shiftings, click of horn against horn when lying close, and the gruntings as one rose to stretch.

Well, right then I had me a healthy hunch, but what I wanted was to locate the fire. I reined my horse over and rode him around a bush, speaking softly so's not to startle the cattle, which, after all, were longhorns and wild animals by anybody's figuring.

The fire was off across the herd, and I glimpsed a faint glow on the side of some leaves over yonder, on a tree trunk. So I let my horse fall into the rhythm of walking around the herd, just as if we were riding night herd ourselves, which we'd done often enough.

From the way my horse acted, I didn't figure these were strange cattle, so when I saw the fire ahead, I rode over and let my horse walk up quiet.

Tyrel, he was a-settin' by the fire, and he never even raised up his head. He just said, "Get down, Tell, we've been a-missin' you."

So I got down and shook his hand, and we Sacketts was together again.

Chapter XIX

"You got yourself some cows," I said.

"Seems as though. We've had some losses. Right now we're a few shy of having nine hundred head. We lost cattle in the stampede, and we lost a few head in the sand hills. All of them are worn down and beat."

"We've got thirty-two head, last count," I told him. Then I asked, "How you fixed for grub?"

"A-plenty. Orrin came along with his carts. Trouble was we under-guesstimated the size of the carts and the appetites of the boys. We'd about decided to go into Fort Carlton to take on more grub."

"Suits me. We've been wishful for coffee the last couple of days, and as for grub, we've been fixin' to chaw rawhide."

"Come daylight," Tyrel said, "we'll move the herd on some fresh grass and go into camp. Give you boys a chance to catch up on your eating."

"How you fixed on ammunition? We've been ridin' scared of a fight."

"We've enough."

The coffee tasted good. We sat by the fire, comparing what had happened to each of us, and we studied some about what Logan's trouble could be.

"Whoever it is that wants our hides," Tyrel said, "is from below the border. At least, those I've talked to. Looks to me like ol' Logan stumbled into something and he's thrown or is about to throw some trouble their way."

When I finished my coffee, I went to my horse and

mounted up. We'd picked a place for meeting that he'd scouted the day before, and I rode back to our camp.

Brandy was standing guard, and I told him of the morning move. "All quiet here," he said. Then he said, "Mr. Sackett? I ain't been punchin' cows long, but there's something that puzzles me. Most of what we've got here are steers, so why do you call them cows?"

"Just a manner of speaking, Brandy. Lots of places you never hear cattle called anything else but cows."

Well, I went in and bedded down, resting easy for the first time in days. Tyrel and Orrin were alive and close by, and tomorrow we'd join up with them. Most of my years I'd lived alone and rode alone; even when I was with other folks, I was usually a man alone. Now my brothers were close by, and it was a comfort.

They'd come a long way. Tyrel had married well and had him a nice ranch.

Orrin's marriage hadn't worked out, but he had studied law, been admitted to the bar, and had been making a name for himself in politics. He was the best educated of us all, and he'd never let up on learning.

We bunched our cattle on a flat among some low hills, and our boys all got together. I noticed Gilcrist had headed for the Ox as soon as the two outfits stopped, and they had them a long talk. Fleming rode nearby a couple of times but did not stop, yet I had an idea they spoke to him.

We started on at daybreak and pushed the cattle at their usual gait. For the first couple of hours, we let them take their time, kind of spread out and grazing; then we moved them along at a steady gait until noontime.

We rested them at noon while we took our turn at coffee and some beef; then we started again with two to three hours of grazing and two to three hours of steady travel until we bedded them down. Driving that way was good for twelve miles a day or better, and we could still keep them in good shape. Naturally, we varied the drives and the grazing in relation to the grass and water.

Me, I was worried. It was unlikely whoever wanted us stopped was going to give up, and the chances were we'd find some tougher men next time.

Also, the country ahead, according to old Baptiste, who had covered it, was rougher and wilder. So far, we had seen few Indians and had no trouble since our meeting with High-Backed Bull, far away in Dakota.

Yet Indians know no borders and roamed where they would, although each tribe had an area it conceived as its own hunting grounds until pushed out by some stronger tribe.

Fort Carlton, or as some termed it, Carlton House, was several days to the north. Leaving there, we must strike westward for the mountains, moving as rapidly as possible considering the condition of the cattle. All this had once been known as Prince Rupert's Land, a vast and beautiful area now in dispute because of Louis Riel's move to set up a provisional government.

We knew little or nothing of the dispute, having learned but the barest details, and had no wish to become involved in something that was clearly none of our business. We had heard there were a few Americans, and no doubt some Canadians as well, hungry for land for themselves or land to sell, who hoped to somehow profit from depriving the *métis* of their lands.

Lin was now the cook, and Baptiste handled the carts and helped with the cooking.

"Have care!" he warned me. "Blackfeet and Cree are fighting, and this is the way they come! They will steal your horses!"

It was a good warning, and we took care, for we had too few horses as it was. We hoped to get more at Carlton, but Baptiste shook his head to indicate doubt.

"Few horse! Many no good!" He paused a minute, then glanced at me. "You ride ver' good. There is a place where some wild horses run, but grizzly bear, too! Much big grizzly! Ver' mean! A place called Bad Hills!"

Day by day, we edged farther north, the length of our drives depending on the grass. In some places, rains had fallen, and the grass grew tall, but we found stretches where grass was poor and water hard to find. There were salt swamps and bare, dry hills. Buffalo we saw in plenty, and there was no question about meat. We found buffalo and occasionally a deer or bighorn sheep.

There were wolves always. They clung to our drive, watching for the chance to pull down any straggler, and several times they succeeded. One of the younger steers went into a swamp to test the water—it was salt—and became mired. Before its frightened bawling could bring us to help, the wolves were upon it.

Tyrel heard and came in at a dead run. His first shot caught one wolf atop the luckless steer and another fled, yelping wildly and dragging its hind quarters. We were too late to help the steer, and Cap put it out of its misery with a bullet.

We were camped at the Bad Hills when trouble erupted suddenly. Brandy had come in for coffee, and Gilcrist sat by the fire with the Ox, preparing to go on night guard.

Brandy was still limping from the fall he had taken during the stampede. Orrin an' me had come in from scoutin', and Orrin was on the ground stripping the gear from his horse. We were back under the trees and out of sight of the camp. Lin was at the fire, and Baptiste was repairing a lariat.

Cap and Haney were coming in; Tyrel, Fleming, and Shorty were with the cattle.

Brandy was limping a little. He'd been thrown and hurt during the stampede but said nothing of it, and we'd never have known except that once in a while, when he'd been in the saddle for a long time, you'd see him favoring the bad leg. Most of us were banged up more or less, but we taken it as part of the day's work, as he did.

It was the Ox who started it. "What's the matter, mama's boy? Tryin' to make somebody think you're hurt?"

"Nothing of the kind. I do my share."

The Ox took up a stick from the pile gathered for the fire. "Where's it hurt, boy? There?" He hit him a crack just below the hip bone.

Brandy turned on him. "You put that stick down, Ox. And you lay off, d'you hear?"

"Or else what?" The Ox sneered.

Orrin came out of the trees. "Or else you settle with me, Ox."

"This is my fight, Mr. Sackett," Brandy said. "I will fight him."

The Ox was twice the size of Brandy and several years older. Orrin walked forward. "Yes, Brandy, you have a prior claim, but this man is working for me, and he has chosen to ignore my suggestions. I'd take it as a favor if you'd let me have him."

"Ha!" The Ox stood up. "Forget it, kid. I'd rather whip this smart lawyer-man. I'll show him something he'll never learn in books!"

He started around the fire, and Orrin let him come. Now I came out of the woods. Cap and Haney rode up, and we saw the Ox start for Orrin, swinging a ponderous right fist. Orrin took a short step off to the left and let the right go over his shoulder. At the same instant, he whipped up his right into the Ox's belly.

It was a jolting punch, but the Ox turned like a cat, dropping into a half crouch. Orrin's left took him in the mouth, but the Ox lunged, grabbing for Orrin to get hold of him. Orrin evaded the clutch, hooked a right to the body, and then walked in quickly with a one-two to the face.

The Ox ducked a left and grabbed Orrin, heaving him from his feet to hurl him violently to the ground. Charging in to put the boots to him, the Ox missed his first kick, and Orrin lunged against the leg on which the Ox was standing. The big man went back and down but came up like a rubber ball. A swinging fist caught Orrin beside the head, and he staggered; a left dug into his midsection, and Orrin clinched with the Ox.

The Ox gave a grunt of satisfaction and wrapped his powerful arms around Orrin and began to squeeze. He was enormously powerful, with arms as thick as the legs of most men, and he put the knuckles of a fist against Orrin's spine; then he spread his legs and brought all his power to bear. Orrin gasped, then hooked a left to the Ox's face, then a right; they had no effect. He started to bend Orrin back, trying literally to break his spine, but Orrin was a veteran of too many mountain and barge fights. He threw up his legs and fell back to the ground, bringing the Ox down atop him. The fall broke the grip the Ox had, and Orrin was too fast. Like an eel, he was out of the bigger man's grasp and on his feet. The Ox lunged and met a stiff left that split his lips. He ducked and tried to get in close, but Orrin put the flat of his hand on the Ox's head and spun him away, then deftly tripped him as the Ox went forward, off balance.

The Ox got up slowly. Orrin, knowing the bigger man was better on the ground, stood back and allowed him to get to his feet. "What's the matter, Ox? Is something wrong?"

Cautious now, the Ox moved in, arms spread wide for grappling. Orrin waited on the balls of his feet, feinted a move to the left, then stepped in with a straight left and a right. The blows jolted the Ox but did not stop him. He landed a light left to Orrin's chest, then a smashing right to the head that made Orrin's knees buckle. Lunging close the Ox's head butted Orrin on the chin, knocking Orrin's head back like it was on a hinge.

Orrin went down. The Ox lunged close, kicking for Orrin's head, but a swift movement partially evaded the kick, taking it on the shoulder. It toppled him over again, and the Ox rushed in, booting Orrin viciously in the ribs. Orrin, gasping with pain, lunged to his feet and swung a left that missed and a right that didn't.

Moving around, neither man showing any sign of weariness, they circled for advantage. Orrin stabbed another left to the Ox's bleeding lips and crossed a right that the Ox ducked under. He smashed a right to the ribs that jolted Orrin, who moved back, stabbing a left to the Ox's face.

The Ox rushed, and instead of trying to evade the rush, Orrin turned sidewise and threw the Ox with a rolling hip lock. The bigger man hit the ground hard, but came up fast, and Orrin threw him again with a flying mare.

Jolted, the Ox got up more slowly, and Orrin moved in, stabbing a left three times to the mouth, then slipping away before the Ox could land.

The Ox was breathing hard now. There was a swelling over his right eye, and his lips were puffed and split. He was learning that he must evade the left that was stabbing at his face. He moved his head side to side with his swaying body, then lunged to come in, lost balance, and as he fell forward, Orrin lifted a knee in his face.

The Ox went to his knees, blood dripping from his broken nose and smashed lips.

There was an awesome power in his huge arms and shoulders, but somehow those fists were always in his face, and Orrin's evasiveness left him helpless. He got up slowly, of no mind to quit. As his hands came up, Orrin's left hit him again, and the right crossed to his chin.

He ducked under another right and hooked a right to Orrin's ribs that seemed to have lost none of its power. Orrin stabbed a left that the Ox evaded. Another left missed and then another. Orrin feinted the same left and landed a jolting right cross. He feinted the left again and repeated with the right. The Ox moved in; Orrin feinted the left and then followed through with a stiff jab to the mouth.

The Ox circled warily waiting for the chance he wanted. He knew his own strength and knew what he could do. He had never fought anyone as elusive as Orrin Sackett, nor anyone who could hit as hard. He was learning there were times when strength was almost useless, but he was in no way whipped. He was getting his second wind, and he was ready. Above all, Orrin seemed to be slowing down.

He no longer could be content with whipping Orrin Sackett. He wanted to maim or kill him. Get hold of an arm or a leg and break it. Break his neck if he could. *Kill him!*

The Ox held his hands low, inviting the jab. Could he grab that darting fist, so like a snake's tongue? If he could—

The fist darted, and he caught it in his open palm. The other palm smashed upward at Orrin's elbow, but instead of resisting, Orrin went with the power and fell forward to his knees. Before he could turn, the Ox booted him in the ribs. He felt a wicked stab of pain, and he lunged to his feet.

Orrin moved carefully. That he had at least one broken rib he was sure. He had narrowly evaded a broken arm or shoulder. The Ox was learning, and he was dangerous. He had to get him out of there, and now.

There could be no delay.

The Ox, suddenly confident, was coming in now, ready to destroy him. Orrin feinted a left, and the Ox smiled. Orrin backed off slowly, and the Ox, sure of himself, came on in. Orrin feinted a left, and the Ox blocked it with almost negligent ease but failed to catch the right that shot up, thumb and fingers spread.

It caught him right under the Adam's apple, drew back swiftly, and struck again just a little higher.

The Ox staggered back, gagging, then went to his knees, choking and struggling for breath.

Orrin backed off a little, then said to Gilcrist, "Take care of him."

He sat down, mopping his brow; then he looked around at me. "They don't come much tougher."

"No," I said, "they surely don't. Better soak those

hands in some warm water with some salts in it. It will take the soreness out."

I walked over to the fire and filled my cup. We had made a good start, but we had a long way to go.

And we were losing two hands.

Chapter XX

We gulped black coffee in the cool, crisp air, then saddled our broncs for the drive. We roused our cattle from their resting place and moved them out on the trail. There were wild, shrill calls from the cowboys then and whoops to hurry them on. There was a click of horns and a clack of hoofs and the bawling of an angry steer, but the cattle bunched up, and old Brindle took the lead and we headed toward Carlton.

We hung their horns on the Northern Star, and the pace was good for an hour, and then we let them graze as they moved.

"Don't bother with Eagle Creek," Baptiste advised. "The water is brackish, although the grass is good. There's a wooded glen beyond, a place of trees and springs. But much grizzlies, too."

By late afternoon, we were crossing a long, gently sloping flat; then we pushed the cattle through Eagle Creek and moved on toward the Bad Hills.

It was one long hill, really, and not so much of one at that, cut with many deep, wooded ravines. I did not wonder there might be bears, for the country suited them. It reminded me somewhat of the canyons in the mountain range back of the Puebla de Los Angeles, in California. I'd been there once, long since, and there were grizzlies there, too.

We saw none of the wild horses Baptiste had told us would be there. Orrin came in with a story of old horse tracks on the far side of the herd and added, "This is Blackfoot country."

Fort Carlton was about a quarter of a mile back

from the river, a palisaded place with bastions at each of the corners. We bunched our cattle on a flat and a hillside not far from the fort, and with Tyrel remaining with the herd, Orrin and I rode in.

We had come some distance from the Bad Hills, a place we were glad to be free of, as we lost two steers there to grizzlies, both of them found in the morning, one half eaten, the other dragged some distance and covered with brush.

There were a good many Indians, all friendly, in the vicinity of Carlton. At the store, where many things were on sale, we arranged to buy a small amount of ammunition and some supplies. More, they suggested, might be available if we talked to the man in charge.

We were coming out of the store when Orrin stopped short. A girl in a neat gray traveling suit came toward him, hands outstretched. "Why, Mr. Sackett! How nice!"

He flushed and said, "Tell, let me introduce you to Devnet Molrone."

"Howdy, ma'am!"

She turned. "And this is Mrs. Mary McCann, Mr. Sackett!"

"Well, well! Howdy, Mrs. McCann!"

Mary McCann had flushed. Nettie glanced at her, surprised, then at me. I hoped my expression showed nothing but pleasure at the meeting.

"Rare pleasure, Mrs. McCann," I said. "Women-folks to a man on the trail—well, we surely see al-mighty few of them. I've got a friend along with me who would be right happy to shake your hand, ma'am, if you was so inclined. I reckon he ain't seen a woman in weeks, maybe months."

Mary McCann looked right at me and said, "Now that's interestin'. I haven't seen many men, either. Just what would his name be?"

"Mr. Rountree? We call him Cap. He's seen most everything a man can see an' been most everywhere, but I d'clare, ma'am, he'd be right proud to meet you!"

Nettie Molrone put her hand on Orrin's sleeve. "Mr. Sackett? My brother is not here, and they are not sure they even remember him! They think he passed through on his way west."

"I was afraid of that, ma'am."

"Mr. Sackett? You're going on west. Could you take me? Take us?"

Orrin glanced at me, hesitating. Now the last person I wanted on a cattle drive was a young, pretty woman. As far as that goes, Mary McCann was a handsome woman, considering her age and poundage.

"Please? There's no other way west, and I *must* find my brother! I have to find him!"

"Well—" I hesitated, trying to find a way out, and I couldn't see one. After all, I was the oldest brother, and officially, I suppose, I was the boss. Not that I wanted the job or cared for it.

All the time, I was wondering what Cap would say and wondering also how Mary McCann got her name and what made her change it. Not that a change of names was anything unusual west of the Mississippi, and especially west of the Rockies. The last time I'd run into Mary McCann was down New Mexico way.

"Ma'am," I said, "it's a far land to which we go, and the way will be hard. Nothing like what you see here. So far as I know, there's but one fort betwixt here and the mountains. The land is wild, ma'am, with Injuns, with wolves and grizzlies.

"We may be long periods without water, and the grub may not be of the best. We can stop for nothing, man, woman, or beast, once we start moving again. We've taken a contract to deliver these cattle before winter sets in, and were bound an' determined to do it.

"If you come with us, we'll play no favorites. You'll stand to the drive as the men do, and at times you may be called upon to help. It is a hard land, ma'am, and we'll have no truck with those who come with idle hands."

Her chin came up. "I can do my share! I will do my share!"

Well, I looked at her, the lift to the chin and the glint in her eyes, and I thought of Orrin there beside her, and I remembered the failure of his first marriage. If this girl stood to it, she was a woman to ride the river with, and Orrin wanted it, and her. Surely, no woman would have a harder time of it.

"All right," I said, "but no whining, no asking for favors. You'll be treated like a lady."

"You need have no fears." She stood straight and looked me in the eye. "I can stand as much as any man."

"Can you ride, ma'am? And can you shoot?"

"I can ride. I can shoot a little."

"Come along, then, and if your brother is alive, we we will find him."

"What became of Kyle Gavin?" Orrin asked.

She frowned a little. "Why, I don't know. He was very attentive, and then suddenly he was there no longer. I don't know when he left or how."

When I went outside, Cap was riding in through the gate with Highpockets Haney. "Cap," I said, "if you see any familiar faces don't call them by name."

He looked at me out of those wise old eyes, eyes wiser and older than the man himself, and he said, "I learned a long time ago that a name is only what a person makes it."

He stepped down and said, "What about those womenfolks?"

"We're takin' them with us, Cap. One of them is tough enough and strong enough to charge hell with a bucket of water. The other one thinks she is."

Cap hesitated, one hand resting on his saddle. "Tell, you and me know better than any of them what lies ahead."

"We do," I said.

We had ridden the empty trails with a hollow moon in the sky and the bare peaks showing their teeth at the sky. We'd seen men die and horses drop, and we'd seen cattle wandering, dazed from thirst and heat. The leather of our hides had been cured on the stem by hot winds and cold, by blown dust and snow and hail falling. We knew what lay ahead, and we knew that girl might die. We knew she might go mad from heat and dust, and we knew I'd no business in letting her come. Yet I'd seen the desperation in her eyes and the grim determination in her mouth and chin.

"Orrin's taken with her, Cap," I said, "and I think she'll stay the route."

"If you say so," he said. He tied his horse. "That person you thought I might put a name to?"

"Mary McCann," I said, "and she's a damned fine cook." I looked at him slyly. "An' for much of her life she's been in love with a miserable old mountain man turned cownurse who drifts where the wind takes him."

"I wouldn't know anybody like that," he said, and went inside.

We got the pemmican and other supplies we needed, including the ammunition, but we couldn't buy them for money. They needed cattle. When we started out of Fort Carlton, we were thirty head short of what we brought in. They wanted the beef, we needed the supplies, and lucky it was because none of us were carrying much money. We'd spent a good bit and were running shy of cash money.

We went over the bluffs and into higher, beautiful pasture land, and we let the cattle graze. God knew what lay before us, but the best advice we got was to fatten our stock whilst we could.

Many a time those days I wished I had the words of Orrin, who could speak a beautiful tongue. It was the Welsh in us, I guess, coming out in him, but it left me saddened for my own lack. I hadn't no words with which to tell of the land, that beautiful green land that lay before and around us. Some didn't like the cotton-woods. Well, maybe they weren't just that for folks up here called them poplars, and maybe that's what they were. Only they were lovely with their green leaves rustling.

Westward we marched, short-handed by two, for we'd left the Ox and Gilcrist behind.

It had all come to a head when we were fixing to leave Carlton. Gilcrist had come to me with the Ox at his shoulder. "We want our time," Gilcrist said.

When he had his money in his hand, Gilcrist said, "Someday I'm goin' to look you up, Sackett. Someday I want to find out if you can really handle that gun."

"Follow me back to the States," I said, "and choose your time."

"To the States? Why the States?"

"I'm a visitor here," I said, "and a man has no call to get blood on a neighbor's carpet."

Westward we went following a route north of the North Saskatchewan through a country of hills and poplars with many small lakes or sloughs. There was no shortage of firewood now, for at every stop we found broken branches under the trees. It was a lovely, green, rolling country even now in the latter days of July.

Anxiously, we watched the skies, knowing that cold came soon in these northern regions and that we had but little time. The nights were cool and the mornings crisp; the campfires felt good.

"A good frost would help us," Cap said, nursing a cup of coffee by the fire, "kill off some of these mosqueeters an' flies."

We were camped by Bear Lake, a place I could have stayed forever. How many times I have found such campsites! Places so beautiful it gave a man the wistfuls to see or to think back on. So many times we said, "We've got to come back some time!" an' knowin' all the while we never would.

That night, we heard the wolves howl, and there were foxes barking right out by the cattle. In the night, we heard a squabble, an' Tyrel an' me came out of our sleep, guns in hand. Then the noise quieted down, and we went back to sleep, only to be awakened again with a wild bawling of a cow, the crack of a whip, and the yelp of a wolf.

Come daylight, we learned some wolves had jumped a steer; he'd been scratched in some brush earlier and had blood on him. Orrin had come in with that Spanish whip he carried on his saddle, a long, wicked lash that could take the hide off. He'd used it on wolves before, and he could flick a fly from a steer's hide without touching the steer. I'd seen him do it.

The steer the wolves had attacked was so badly hurt it had to be shot.

We were breaking camp when we heard some yells, then a sound of galloping horses. In a moment, we had our rifles, but Baptiste gestured wildly and waved us back.

It was a party of *métis* wearing brass-buttoned capots, calico shirts in a variety of colors, and moleskin trousers. Their belts were beaded in red and white or blue and white, and most of them wore cloth caps, only a few having hats and one a coonskin cap.

They were a friendly, cheerful lot, talking excitedly with Baptiste whom they obviously knew well.

"They go to Fort Pitt," he explained. "They are hunters, and they have been to another camp, feasting."

Tyrel indicated their horses. "Wish we had some of them. That's some of the best horseflesh I've seen."

When Baptiste suggested it, they agreed to show us some stock when we reached Fort Pitt. After drinking an enormous amount of coffee, they swung to their saddles and dashed off, whooping and yelling, at top speed.

After they had gone, Baptiste stopped me as I was mounting. "Bad!" he whispered. "Ver' bad! They speak of many mans, maybe ten, twelve mans near Jackfish Lake. They wait for somebody, or somet'ing. Today, they say the mans move back into woods, hide horses."

Haney came in for coffee at the nooning. "Seen

some tracks. Two riders, keepin' out of sight. I caught a flash of sunlight on a rifle and slipped around and taken a look. They're scoutin' us."

"White men?"

"You betcha! Well mounted, Tell, well mounted an' well armed."

Well, we had known it was coming. Now we were in wild country. If we vanished out here, who would know? Or care?

Chapter XXI

no sneaking up.

wanted to come up, out in the night, they

Wolves hung on our flanks as we moved out, nor would they be driven off. We had no wish to shoot and attract undue attention, nor would the waste of ammunition have done any good, for their ranks were continually added to by other wolves.

We pushed on over some flat country dotted by trees and groups of trees, crossing several small streams.

It was the thought of a stampede that worried me. "If they scatter our stock, we lose time in the gather," I said. "Cap? Why don't you scout on ahead and try to find us a camp in the woods? Some place where we can fall some trees to make a so-so corral?"

"I can look," he said.

"Ride easy in the saddle," I said. "This is an ugly bunch. I don't think much of them as fightin' men, but they'll kill you."

He rode off through the scattered trees, and we came on. Fleming was doing a good day's work, but I still had no trust in the man. There had seemed to be something between him an' Gilcrist.

Nettie was proving herself a hand. She caught on to what was necessary, and she rode well. I'd no doubts about Mary McCann. She might be no youngster, and she might be carrying some weight, but she could still ride most anything that wore hair.

We pushed on, and I had to smile at Haney and Shorty. Both of them were pretty handy with the cussing, but since the girls showed up, there was none of that. It must have been a strain, but they were bearing up under it.

Cap had us a camp when we came to it, a small meadow near a stream with trees and brush all around. We watered them, got them inside, and dragged some deadfalls across the openings. Then we scouted the brush and trees on both sides to see how an attacker might approach us.

Cap an' me, we went back in the trees and rigged some snares and deadfalls, traps for anybody who might come sneaking up.

If they wanted to come up on us in the night, they were asking for whatever they got. Come daylight, we'd dismantle the traps so's they wouldn't trap any unwary man or animal after we'd gone.

Lin fixed us a mighty nice supper, having a mite more time. Nettie came to me while we were eating. "Why can't we stand watch? You men need the rest."

"Let them," Cap was saying.

None of us had been around when Cap finally met Mary, and none of us asked any questions, although I was curious as to what made her change her name and leave that place she had back in New Mexico. But it was her business. By the position of the Big Dipper, it was maybe two o'clock in the morning when Nettie touched me on the shoulder. "There's something moving in the brush," she said, "several somethings."

She and Mary had been riding herd, and I rolled out, shook out my boots, and stuck my feet into them. Haney was already moving, and so were Orrin and Tyrel.

Taking up my Winchester I followed her to her pony. He was standing head up, looking toward the woods, his ears pricked. At just that moment, there was a sudden crash in the brush and a grunt, then an oath.

"Sit tight, boys," I said. "Don't go into the woods."

Somebody called for help in a low voice, but there was no answer; then there was some threshing about, we all just awaiting to see what would happen.

Nothing did until suddenly there was a louder crash and some swearing.

"Nettie," I whispered, "you and Mary might as well get some sleep."

"And miss all the fun?"

Me, I taken a long look at her. "Ma'am," I said, "if anything happens, it won't be fun. It will be hard times for somebody, probably them. You get some sleep whilst you've the chance."

Turning to Orrin, I said, "You an' Tye go back to sleep. Me an' Highpockets can handle this here."

"You figure we caught something?"

"By the sound, we caught two somethings," I said, "and I suspect we've persuaded them that crawlin' in the brush ain't what they want to do."

When day was breaking, we stirred up the fire for Lin and Highpockets and me; we decided to see what we'd caught and whether it needed skinning or not.

We come to a snare, and there we had a man hangin' head down by one ankle, and he was some unhappy. He'd been hangin' there several hours, and he had been mad; now he was almost cryin' to be set loose.

Me an' Haney, we looked at him. "The way I figure it, Haney," I said, "anything catched in a trap has fur, and when something has fur, you skin it for the hide."

"I know," he said. "That's the way we always did it in the mountains, but this one's kind of skimpy on the fur." He took the man by his hair and tilted his face up. "He's got fur on his lip. Maybe we should skin that like I hear you done to somebody down New Mexico way."

I reached over and taken him by the end of his handlebar moustache. I held his head up by it while he swung widly with his arms. Haney hit one of the wrists a crack with the barrel of his pistol, and the swings stopped.

Holding him by the end of his moustache I turned his head this way and that.

"No," I said, "I don't think it's worth skinning. I figure we should just let him hang. Maybe somebody will come for him."

"Nobody has," Haney said. "Give him a few days and he'll dry out some."

The man's pistol had fallen to the ground, and Haney picked it up, then unstrapped the man's cartridge belt. "Would you look at this here, Tell? This man's been walkin' in the dark woods with a pistol in his hand. Why, he might have hurt somebody!"

"Or tripped over something and shot hisself. We'd better carry that gun with us so's he won't get hurt."

Haney walked around the hanging man, looking him over. "How long d'you think a man could hang like that?"

"Well"—I pushed my hat back and scratched my head—"depend on how long before some bear found him, or maybe the wolves. If they stood on their hind legs, they could sure enough reach him.

"Man smell would bother them for a while," I suggested. "Then they'd get over that and start jumpin' for him. Sooner or later, one of them would get hisself a piece of meat—"

"Hey! You fellers goin' to let me hang here, or are you goin' to turn me loose?"

"It talks," Haney said, "makes words like it was almost human. How d'you think anything got caught in a trap like that?"

"Must've been sneakin' in the woods," I said. "We'd better let this one hang an' see what else we got."

"Aw, fellers! Come on now! Turn a man loose!"

"So you can come huntin' us again?" Haney asked. "No way."

We walked off through the woods toward the deadfall.

There was no game in that trap, but there had been. There was a hat lying on the ground, but the victim had been carried away. We could see tracks where two men had helped a third away. "Busted a leg, most likely," Haney suggested cheerfully. "Lucky it wasn't his skull."

Our other traps were empty, so we dismantled them and went back to camp. "They don't know much,"

Haney said, "but they'll learn from their troubles. Or maybe they'll recruit some all-out woodsman who could make trouble for us."

He paused. "Shall we just forget about that other feller?"

"We don't want him hangin' arround," I suggested, "so let's turn him loose."

We done so. And when he had his feet on the ground, I told him to take off his boots.

"What?"

"Take off your boots," I said, "and your pants. We need something for the fire."

"Now see here! I—!"

"Give him a short count," I said to Haney, "and if he ain't got his boots off, shoot him."

He stared at me, wild-eyed, then hit the ground and tugged off his boots. "Now your pants," I said.

He took off his pants. I shook my head at him. "You ought to wash them long johns. Ain't decent, a man as dirty as that." I pointed off through the woods. "Your friends, if you've got any, are off thataway. You get started."

"Now look here," he protested, "that's a good set of spurs! I wish—"

"Beat it," I said. "You take off through those woods and don't you ever come back. If I see you out here again, I'll hang your hide on the nearest deadfall."

"Those are good spurs," Haney said.

"Hang 'em on a tree," I said. "Somebody will find them."

We bunched our cows and started them west, and we swung south to avoid the traveled trails. We found fair pasture and moved them along. The wolves taken a steer here and there, and we lost one to a grizzly. Shorty nailed the grizzly but not before he'd killed a good-sized steer.

The grass was sparse, and we crossed some sandy plains with occasional low hills. We had to scout for patches of good grass, but it looked like forest was taking over from the plains. On the third day after the mix-up in the trees, we saw a party of riders coming toward us, but Baptiste told us they were *métis,* and sure enough they were.

Some of them were the same crowd we'd met, and they brought some horses for trading. We had them with us all night and most of the next day, but when we split up, we had nine good horses and a couple of fair ones, and they had some odds and ends of truck as well as some cash money.

We swapped them a rifle we'd picked up and the pistol we'd taken from our hanging man, among other things. The Canadian army had come to Fort Garry, they said, and Riel had disappeared before they could lay hands on him.

The *métis* wanted sugar, salt, and tobacco, and I had an idea they were hiding out themselves, although they were a far piece from Fort Garry now. Evidently, they planned to stay out of sight for a while. With salt, coffee, and tobacco, they could live off the country. It was their country, and they understood it well.

They warned us we were going into wild country where there was little grass and no trails for cattle.

We pushed on regardless, and for the first time our worn-down saddle stock got a rest.

Before they parted from us, one of the *métis* who was a friend to Baptiste and had become my friend, also, took me aside and warned me.

"Two mans, ver' bad. They come to Fort Garry and ride to Carlton. They are sent for by a bearded man, and they meet two other mans who come from the States who are brothers, also. They hunt for you."

"The first two men? Do you know who they are?"

"*Oui.* Ver' bad! Polon is their name. Pete and Jock Polon. If the Hudson's Bay Company was here, they would not come back! They are thieves! They killed trappers! They killed some Cree! And in the woods they are superb! Have a care, *mon ami!* Have a care!"

We drove on another seven miles before we camped after watching the *métis* ride away.

Orrin looked across the campfire at me that night.

"Tell, we aren't going to make it. We can't make it before snow flies."

"What d'you think, Cap?"

"Orrin's right. We've got to push them, Orrin, even if we run beef off them. After all, it's cattle we are supposed to deliver. Nobody said nothing about fat cattle!"

That night, two men, headed east, rode into our camp. "You're takin' *cattle* out there?" They stared at me. "You must be crazy!"

"You mean there's no market?"

"Market? Of course, there's a market! It's gettin' 'em there. There's no decent trails; there's rivers to cross, grizzlies a-plenty, and wolves—you ain't seen any wolves yet!"

One of them, a tall man named Pearson, indicated the carts. "You won't be able to use those much longer. The trails are too narrow. Put your stuff on pack horses."

"My old horse will carry a pack," Brandy suggested. "He's done it before."

We sat long with the two travelers, getting as much advice as we could. They drew the trail in the dirt for us, indicating the passes.

"How are things up there?" I asked. "Peaceful?"

"Generally speaking Some of the boys get a mite noisy now and again. There's brawls and such and once in a great while a shooting. Mostly, they're just noisy."

"The best claims are all taken," the other one said. "If you're figuring on staking claims, forget it."

"We'll just sell our beef and get out," Orrin commented. Then, tentatively, he added, "We promised delivery to a man named Sackett, Logan Sackett."

They stared at him. "Too bad about him, and I'm afraid you're too late. He's dead."

"What?"

"I'll say this for him. He was a man. Party got trapped in the passes last year, and he went up and brought 'em out. Saved seven men and a woman. He brought 'em through snow like you never saw. Avalanche country."

"You say he's dead?" I asked.

"He went north. There were rumors of a strike up in the Dease River country. Story was that he was killed in a gun battle up there with some outlander."

"Big man?"

"Your height," Pearson said to Orrin, "but heavier by twenty pounds. Come to think of it, he favored you somewhat."

"Who killed him?"

"That was a bad outfit. They'd been in some trouble in Barkerville. Don't recall what. Five or six of them, and smart, tough men. The one who seemed to be the leader was named Gavin."

"Gavin?" I glanced over at Nettie, who was listening.

"Kyle Gavin?"

"No, this one's called Shanty. Shanty Gavin, and he's as mean and tough as he is smart."

Pearson looked over at me. "It was Shanty Gavin who killed Logan Sackett. Shot him dead."

165

Chapter XXII

Logan Sackett dead? I didn't believe it. He was too durned ornery to die. Besides, I'd seen him come through cuttings and shootings and clubbings like he was born to them.

Shanty Gavin? Any relation to Kyle Gavin?

Who was Shanty, and what did he want? For that matter, who was Kyle Gavin?

Pearson and his partner headed on east, back to the fleshpots and away from the gold fields. Fraser River gold was too fine, and the Cariboo was played out, or so they said, but we'd learned long ago to discount anything anybody said who was either going to or coming from a gold field.

"Any way you look at it," Cap said, "we're drivin' these cows right into trouble."

"I never seen any trouble a cow couldn't handle," Haney said wryly. "What I'm wonderin' about is us. What are we gettin' into?"

"Move 'em along," I said. "The time's gettin' short, and if we don't hurry, there'll be frost on the punkin before we get where we're going."

"I want to get there," Shorty said, "so's we can get out before the snow settles down. I'm a warm-weather man myself, born for the sunny side of the hill."

That was the night we left our carts behind. We divided what they contained into packs for four horses.

"We can burn them," Fleming said. "They'll make a hot fire for cooking."

"We'll leave them," I said. "Somebody may come who needs a cart. We'll push them back under the

166

trees and leave them for whoever comes. Good hands made them, and I'll not destroy honest work."

Again we moved out, pointing our way into the darker hills. The forest was changing now, and ahead of us we saw peaks that were bare of growth, and some were covered by snow. Grass was scarce, and we watched for meadows where the cattle could stop and feed. Our travel was arranged to make the most of grass when we found it There were firs among the poplars now and sometimes groves of stunted pine. We skirted a forest blown down by winds where the dead trees lay in rows like mowed grain.

Orrin was riding point when we met the grizzly. We'd been coming along a forest trail, the cattle strung out for a couple of miles or more and Orrin riding quiet, making no sound. Suddenly, the grizzly arose from the brush and stood tall in the trail. Startled, Orrin's horse reared, and Orrin kept his seat, drawing his pistol as he did so.

The first we knew of trouble was the sharp bark of his pistol, then three times more, rapid fire. Tyrel, Haney, Cap, an' me, we lit out for the front of the column.

Ever try to get through a trail jammed with cattle? It took time, too much time.

Cattle began bucking and plunging, trying to get into the woods and brush on either side of the trail, and we could hear the roaring and snarling of what was obviously a mighty big bear We fought our way through, but getting there was tough

We heard two more shots, and we broke through to find a big grizzly lying in the trail, crippled but still full of fight.

Orrin was just getting up off the ground. His hat was gone, and his buckskin jacket was ripped, and there was blood on his shoulder. He made it to his feet, staggered, and commenced jamming loads into his pistol. Me, I took my rifle from the scabbard and killed that grizzly with two good shots.

He would have died from Orrin's shots, we later saw.

Two of them had hit him in the neck, and after going down, Orrin got two more shots into his spine, fired as the bear was turning. They had crippled him in the hindquarters, which kept him from getting at Orrin. He'd hit him one glancing swipe, knocking him tail over teakettle into the brush.

It taken us the rest of the evening to skin out that grizzly and get the best cuts of meat; then we had to get the cattle around the blood in the trail. The carcass we hauled off with that old plow horse of Brandy's.

Scouting ahead, Shorty found a long meadow along a winding stream, and we turned the cattle in there for a good bit of grass and water. We rounded up some of the cattle that got away into the trees, but there was a few of them we never did find and didn't take the time to hunt. One old steer came up the trail after us when we started the next morning.

All the following day we struggled through bogs, the cattle floundering and plunging, our horses doing no better, and the trail when it could be found at all was wide enough for one animal only. During the whole day, we made scarcely four miles, yet the next morning we climbed a low hill and then another and emerged in a forest of huge old poplars, scattered but with no undergrowth. Here and there, the cattle found a bite of something, usually a clump of wildflowers. We made good time and by nightfall had twelve miles of easy travel behind us.

We broke out into a plain at sundown, and the cattle scattered on the good grass there, and we found a camp up against some willows and near a small stream.

We were dead beat, and me an' Shorty were taking the first guard. I slapped a saddle on a dusty red roan and cinched up. I was putting my rifle in the scabbard when suddenly there was a thunder of hoofs, wild shrill whoops, and we saw a party of Indians swooping down upon us.

I grabbed my rifle back out of the scabbard, saw

Tyrel hit the dirt behind a log, and heard Haney's pistol barking, and then they were gone and with them about fifty head of our cattle.

Well, I done some cussing, then apologized to Nettie, who came up from the campfire to see what had happened.

"Blackfeet," Cap said. "Count yourself lucky they wasn't war minded."

"Let's go get 'em!" Shorty suggested.

Cap just glanced at him, but that glance said more than a passel of words. "Blackfeet, I said. You don't chase Blackfeet, Shorty. You just count your blessings an' let 'em go.

"Those were young braves, just out for a lark. They wasn't huntin' scalps, but you go after them, and they will. We lost some cows. Let's move out of here."

"To where?"

"Any place but here. They might get to thinkin' on it and come back."

Tired as we were, we put out our fire, loaded our gear, and headed off up the trail. We found a meadow three miles farther on and bedded them down.

Nobody set by the campfire that night; nobody wanted a second cup of coffee. Everybody crawled into his bed, and only the night guard was left.

Day after day, we plodded on; we had lost cattle one way or another until at least a third of them were gone. Old Baptiste killed a mountain sheep, and we dined well, but it had been weeks since we had seen a buffalo. There was little talk now during the day. Fleming looked sour and discontented. He seemed to have been expecting something that did not happen.

"Overlanders have come this way," Cap said, "but it's been a while."

All the tracks we found were old, and we were getting more and more worried.

"Beats me where we're to meet Logan, if he's alive."

"That feller said he was dead," Fleming said, "that he'd been killed."

"He's a hard man to kill."

"A bullet will do it for anybody," Fleming said. "If he's hit in the right place, one man is no tougher than another."

"Seems like we've been pushin' these cows forever," Shorty said. "I wouldn't mind standin' up to a bar for a drink."

"Be a while," Tyrel said. "You boys set easy. Goin' back will be easy as pie."

"If we ever," Fleming said.

Nettie and Mary had been keeping out of the way. They knew this was a trying time, and they had done their best to help. Both of them had become good hands, although Mary—well, she'd been *born* a hand.

"If my brother is out here," Nettie asked Orrin, "where do you think he would be?"

Orrin shrugged. "There's Barkerville, and there's Clinton. I don't know many of the towns, but I can tell you this. If he's in this country or has been, some of those folks will know. This is a big country, but she's right scarce of people. A body can be away up yonder at the forks of the creek, and somebody will have seen him. There's nothing happens up here somebody doesn't know about."

Fleming chuckled. It was a dry, rather unpleasant, skeptical chuckle. Nobody said anything.

We'd been keeping our eyes open for sign. All three of us Sacketts expected it, and we knew the sort of sign one Sackett was apt to leave for another.

We found nothing.

We waded rivers, fourteen crossings in one day, and wove our way through some fir trees whose wet branches slapped us wickedly as we passed. The horses were game. They struggled through the muskeg, and finally we topped out on some reasonably solid ground.

Supplies were running low, and game was scarce. All day we had seen nothing. Ducks flew over, the Vs of their flight pattern pointing south. In the morning when we awaken, there was a chill in the air.

"Wonder what become of those Injuns we had followin' us?" Cap asked one day. "I kind of miss 'em?"

"Little Bear," I said, "now there was a lad."

"If we don't get something to eat soon," Lin suggested, "we'll have to slaughter a beef."

Now there's little goes more against the grain of a good cattleman than killing his own beef. But we'd left buffalo country behind, and we were fresh out of bear. Me, I was of no mind to tackle a grizzly unless he came hunting trouble, which they often did. A grizzly has been king in his own world for so long, he resents anybody coming around. Only man threatens his world, and whether he avoids or fights men depends pretty much on his mood at the moment.

Down San Francisco way during the gold rush, some of the gamblers used to pit bears in cages with lions, tigers, and most anything that would fight. The grizzly almost always won in quick time. In one particular case, a full-grown African lion lasted less than three minutes.

There were a lot of grizzlies in these mountains, but mostly they kept out of the way, not because they were afraid, but because they simply did not want to be bothered.

Orrin, who reads a lot, was reading me a piece in a magazine, *Century* or *Atlantic,* I think, about some explorers coming back from some foreign country where they'd been hunting some wild creature. They were busy hunting for a few weeks and came back saying there was no such thing. Now I've lived in panther or mountain lion country most of my life and never seen but one or two that weren't treed by hounds. Wild animals don't want to be seen, and it's sheer accident if you see them.

We were climbing all the while, getting higher and higher, and the nights were getting colder. Then, one morning, Tyrel come to me. "Tell," he said, there's a fringe of ice on the lake, yonder."

Well, that sent a chill through me. A fringe of ice—and we had some distance to go. I wasn't sure how much.

Now we were moving up some magnificent valleys, green and lovely with great walls of mountain rising on either side; often these were sheer precipices of bare rock, or with an occasional tree growing from some rock a body could no way get to. We caught fish, and one night I got three ducks in three shots with a rifle, two sitting, one just taking off. They were needed, as grub was getting low. We had flour, salt, and the like, but we needed meat.

Every morning now there was frost. The sky was gray often enough, and one night, when there were no clouds, we saw the Northern Lights, a tremendous display brightening the whole heavens. I'd heard of it but seen it but once before, in Montana, but never like this.

It was late afternoon, and Tyrel was riding point. It was an easy trail, across some green meadows and up along a trail through huge boulders and scattered clumps of fir. Me, I was riding on the flank when I saw Tyrel pull up short.

Well, my rifle snaked into my hands, and I saw Cap Rountree out with his, but Tyrel wasn't drawing. He was looking at a big gray boulder beside the trail.

Coming down off the slope, I rounded the head of the herd and pulled up alongside him. I started to say, "What's wrong, Tye?" and did say it before I looked past him and saw the mark on the face of the boulder.

Scratched on the face of the rock was **CLINCH-S-Dease-?**

"Well," Orrin had come up, "he isn't dead then."

"Who isn't dead?" It was Fleming.

Orrin an' Tyrel glanced at me, and I said, "We're losin' time, boys. We've got a far piece to go."

Fleming stared hard at the scratching on the rock.

172

"What's that mean?" he wondered. "It don't make no sense!"

"Doesn't, does it?" Tyrel said mildly. He turned his mount. "Hustle them along, Charlie. We've a ways to go."

Reluctantly, Charlie Fleming turned away.

Nettie Molrone rode up with Mary McCann. "What is it, Orrin?"

"Just some scratching on a rock," he said. "We were wondering about it, that's all."

She looked at him quickly, her eyes searching his. She glanced at the rock. "It doesn't make sense. Except"—she paused, studying it—"there's a Dease River up here somewhere and a Dease Lake."

"There is?" Orrin looked surprised. "What d'you know about that?"

She looked at him again, half angry.

In the morning, Charlie Fleming was gone.

173

Chapter XXIII

Fleming was gone, and a light rain was falling that froze as it reached the ground. We drank our coffee standing around the hissing fire in our slickers.

"I'd like to know where he went," Orrin said, "but it's not worth following him."

"D'you think he made sense out of Logan's message?"

"If he did," Shorty said, "he's smarter than me."

"We've been passing messages around for years," Orrin said. "Started back in the feuding days, I reckon. The 'Clinch S' just means he's a Clinch Mountain Sackett, which is one branch of the family, descended from old Yance. 'Dease?' simply means we should head for the Dease River, and the destination after that is in doubt."

"Unless you were one of the family," Tyrel commented, "it's unlikely you'd guess."

"Why'd you say he was still alive? That message might have been written days ago."

"Could be, but it's scatched on there with some of that chalk rock he picked up, and had it been more'n a few days old, it would have washed away."

Cap came riding in as they were mounting. "Took a look at the trail," he said. "There's a marker there. Could be by one of you boys, but that trail is one thin cow wide, and with this ice—"

"Think we can make it?"

"Maybe. There's no tellin' the luck of a lousy cow. Anyway, it doesn't seem like we have much choice."

"It's up to me, then," I said, and rode out with old Brindle falling in behind.

When we started up the trail, old Brindle hesitated, not liking it. His horns rattled against the wall, but as I was going on, and he was used to following, he sort of fell in behind.

"Hope I don't let you down, old boy," I said. "It looks bad to me, too!"

We wound steadily upward, the trail narrowing, then widening, occasionally opening to a small space of an acre or more covered with stunted trees, then narrowing again. The sleet continued to fall, and the air was cold. Far below, we could see the spearlike tops of trees, and the silver ribbon of a stream.

The trail grew steeper. At times, I had to dismount and lead my mount over the icy rocks. At one point, I came to a bank of last year's snow, a dirty gray shelf of the stuff, which I had to break off to make a way for my horse and the following cattle.

It was slow, hard work. All day long, we climbed. There was no place to stop and rest; there was not even a place to stop.

Suddenly, the trail dipped down around a steep elbow bend, and the rock of the trail slanted toward the outer edge. Walking along the wall as tightly as possible, I led the roan around the corner.

The cattle came on. Glancing back when several hundred yards farther along, I was in time to see a steer suddenly slip and, legs flailing, plunge off into space headed for the tops of the trees five hundred feet below. Even as I looked, another fell.

Swearing softly, I plodded on, feeling for footholds around the edge. Suddenly, as it had begun, the narrow trail ended and gave out into a thick forest. Ahead, there was a meadow and beyond a stream, already icing over.

There was room enough, and there was but little undergrowth. Tying the roan, I went to a deadfall and from under it tried to gather some scraps of bark that had not been soaked by the rain. From inside my shirt, I took a little tinder that I always kept for the purpose, and breaking a tuft of it free, I lit a fire. As it blazed up, I hastily added more fuel.

Walking back into the woods, I broke off some of the small suckers that grew from the tree trunks and died. They had long been dead and were free from rain. By the time the cattle began to wander out on the meadow and the first rider appeared, I had a fine fire blazing and was rigging a lean-to between two trees that stood about ten feet apart.

The trees had lower limbs approximately the same height above the ground, and selecting from among the fallen debris, broken limbs, and dead branches one of proper length I rested it in the crotches of the limbs selected, and then I began gathering other sticks to lean slant-wise from the pole to the ground.

From time to time I stopped to add fuel to the fire, well knowing the effect the fire would have on the tired men and the two women.

Across the poles, I put whatever lay to hand. I was not building anything but a temporary shelter, and I used slabs of bark from fallen trees, fir branches and whatever was close by.

By the time Lin and Baptiste reached the fire with the pack horses, I had a fairly comfortable shelter and was starting on another. Haney was first to reach the fire, and he began gathering fir boughs from nearby trees.

Orrin helped Nettie from her horse, and for a moment she swayed and fell against the horse. She straightened up. "I'm sorry," she said. "I guess I'm tired."

One by one, the men came in, carrying their gear, which they dropped under the second shelter. Several of them went to the fire. Cap walked out and began gathering boughs, and after a minute Shorty went to help.

Highpockets Haney held his hands to the fire. He

looked around at me. "Tell Sackett I been a lot of places with you, but if you think I'm goin' back over that trail in the snow, you got another think a-comin'."

"We lost some stock, Cap?"

Rountree looked at me. Tired as he had to be, he looked no different than always. He had degrees of toughness nobody had ever scratched. "That we did!"

Shorty looked over at me. "Fourteen, fifteen head, Tell. I'm sorry."

"This weather's rough," Haney added. "We'll lose some more if we've far to go."

We huddled about the fire, and soon the smell of coffee was in the air. Tyrel went back to the edge of camp, and soon he came in with several chunks of meat. "Big horn," he said. "I nailed him back on the other side of the mountain."

Soon the smell of broiling meat was added to that of coffee. Outside, the falling sleet rustled on the fir boughs and on the meadow. The cattle ceased to eat, and one by one took shelter under the trees.

"Ain't nothin' like a fire," Cap said, "and the smell of coffee boilin'."

"How far you reckon it is" Shorty asked.

Nobody answered because nobody knew. Me, I leaned my forehead on my crossed arms and hoped there would be a marker on this side of the pass we'd come over. We would surely need it because I had no idea which way to turn.

The Dease was someplace off to the northwest. Beyond that, anybody's guess was as good as mine, and I was ramrodding this outfit.

We had fire, and we had shelter, and we had a bit of meat, and good meat at that. Yet I was uneasy.

Where had Charlie Fleming gone?

Surely, as we drew closer and closer to our destination, we drew closer to his also, so why hadn't he waited a bit longer where he could have coffee and grub on the way?

Maybe, just maybe, because we were closer than we thought.

Certainly, even though he could not interpret the message, he would know there had been a message, and that would mean that Logan Sackett was not only alive but free—or probably free.

Had he fled to warn someone of our coming? Or was he afraid of Logan?

Orrin got up and moved over to where Nettie Molrone was. I could hear the murmur of their voices as they talked. "I'll ask about for your brother," he said, "as soon as we meet anybody. There'll be a town," he added, "or something of the kind."

The sleet still fell, but it was changing into snow, which would be worse, for beneath the snow there would be ice on the trails. Beyond the reach of the fire shadows flitted wolves.

Now stories came to me, stories told me when I was a small boy by my father. My father had trapped these very lands; he told us much of animals and their habits and of how the wolves would work as a team to drive an animal or a group of animals into a position where they could easily be killed. To drive an elk or moose out on the ice where he would slip and fall was one trick often used. Sometimes they herded them into swamps or drove them off cliffs.

These tricks were often attempted with men, and the unwary were trapped by them.

The snow continued to fall throughout the night, and when morning came, the ground and the trees were covered with it. We got out of bed under the lean-tos, and Baptiste had a fire built up in no time. It had burned down to coals during the last hours of the morning.

It was good to hear the crackle of the fire and to smell the wood burning. Tyrel saddled up, and him and me took a turn through the woods, bunching the cattle a little. They'd had tolerable shelter under the trees, but it was right cold that morning, and they were in no way anxious to move. Some of the horses had pawed away the snow to get at the grass. These were mustangs, used to wild country and to surviving in all kinds of weather.

We were slow getting started because everybody rolled out a mite slower than usual. Nettie's face looked pinched and tight, and she held her hands to the fire.

Orrin said, "We're gettin' close. This is the kind of country you'll find your brother in."

"How can he stand it? I mean even if there's gold."

"Gold causes folks to do all manner of unlikely things, ma'am," Tyrel said. "Sometimes even folks a body has figured were right good people have turned ugly when gold's in the picture."

"Kyle Gavin did not want me to come looking for my brother," Nettie said. "He offered to lend me the money to start home."

"It's a rough country, ma'am. He knows that. He probably didn't want you to get trapped in a place you couldn't get out of."

We came down to a deep canyon before we'd gone more than a few miles and wound down a narrow switchback trail to the water's edge. The river flowed past the road a whole lot faster than we liked, so we pointed the herd upstream and started them swimming across somewhat against the current. They held to it only a little, but by that time they were well on their way, and when they turned a bit on the downstream side, they were pointed toward the landing. We got most of them across and started up the trail opposite. Shorty was in the lead, and as he topped out on the ridge, we heard a sharp report that went echoing down the canyon, and we saw Shorty whip around in his saddle and fall.

At least two hundred cattle were on the trail, and there was no way to get past them. We urged them on, and they began to boil over the edge, running. We crowded the rest of them across and Tyrel an' me, we

179

went hightailing it up the trail after those cows.

We went over the edge, running, but saw nothing but an empty meadow scattered with the arriving cattle. Shorty's horse stood a short distance off, and Shorty was on the ground. Tyrel rode hellbent for election across the meadow and into the trees, and I swung my horse around and rode to Shorty. He was on his face, and there was a big spot of blood on his back, and I turned him over easy.

His eyes were open, and he said, "Never saw him, Tell. Not even a glimpse. Sorry."

He was hit hard, and he knew it. Nettie came up over the rim followed by Mary, and they went right to him.

"I did my part, Tell. Didn't I?" He stared up at me.

"All any man could, Shorty. We rode some rivers together."

"It ain't so bad," he said. "There's nobody to write to. I never had nobody, Tell."

"You had us, Shorty, and when we ride over the rim, we'll be lookin' for you. Keep an eye out, will you?"

There were low clouds, and the place where he lay was swept clean of snow. Nettie and Mary, they came to him, trying to ease him some, as womenfolk will.

"Can't you do something, Tell?" Nettie said to me.

"Nothin' he can do, ma'am," Shorty said. "Just don't try to move me."

Tyrel came back from the woods, and Orrin rode up, and we squatted near Shorty. "Highpockets and me," Shorty said, "we were headin' for the Jackson Hole country. You tell him he'll have to go it alone, will you?"

"He's comin', Shorty. He'll be here in just a moment."

"He better hurry. I got my saddle on something I can't ride."

Highpockets loomed over them. "See you down the

road a piece, Shorty. You be lookin' for me. You'll know me because I'll have a scalp to my belt."

Nettie brushed the hair back from his brow, and Shorty passed with his eyes on her face.

"He was a man loved high country," I said. "We'll bury him here."

"Smoke over yonder," Cap said. "Might be a town."

"Bunch the cattle," I said. "We're going on in."

Chapter XXIV

Of the cattle with which we started less than half remained, and they were lean and rangy from the long drive.

"Nettie," Orrin advised, "you and Mrs. McCann had better hang back behind the herd. We're going to have trouble."

"What's this all about, anyway?" Mary McCann demanded.

"We'll know when we meet Logan, and that should be soon."

"Is that a town down there?"

"It is no town," Baptiste said. "Once there was fort. A man named Campbell had fort here back in 1838 or '39. Sometimes trapper mans camped here."

"There's somebody here now," Haney said, "and somebody killed Shorty."

Sitting my roan horse, I listened to what was being said with only a bit of my attention. What was worrying me was what we'd find down below. Shorty had been killed. Shot right through the chest and spine and shot dead. He had been shot deliberately, and to me it looked like they were trying to warn us to stay out.

"Baptiste? Why here? Why don't they want us there? Why would anybody want a herd of cattle here? There isn't enough grass to keep a herd of this size alive."

"You say he say 'before winter comes.' They want beef. They want food. No game comes in winter. Ver' little game. People could be much hungry.

"Winter comes an' nobody here. Nobody goes out. I

t'ink somebody wish to stay here through the winter."

"He could be right, Tell," Orrin said. "What other answer is there?"

"Whoever it is, they mean business. The shooting of Shorty was deliberate. It was a warning. *Stay out or be killed.*"

Suddenly, I made up my mind. My impulse was to go right on in, but into what? "We'll camp," I said. "We'll camp right here on the mountain."

Tyrel turned to stare at me. "I say let's go on in. Let's get it done."

"Get what done, Tye? Who is the enemy? Who are we hunting? Where's Logan? If he's free, he may not even be down there. If he's a prisoner, we'd better know where he is.

"There may be ten men down there, and there may be fifty. They've already showed us they are ready to fight, and to kill. According to what we heard, they've got the Samples down there and those Polon brothers.

"Go into camp," I said, "right back at the edge of the trees, and let's get set for a fight."

We moved the cattle into a kind of a cul de sac at the edge of the forest. Dragging a log into place here and there and propping them against trees, we made a crude sort of a fence. It wouldn't stop a determined steer but might stop a casual wanderer.

We found a place at the edge of the trees where a fire might safely be built without being seen from too great a distance. "Fix us a good meal, Lin," I suggested. "We may need it tomorrow."

"What's on your mind, Tell?"

"I'm going down there tonight. I'm going to see what's going on."

"They will expect somebody."

"Maybe."

"If Logan didn't leave that marker himself," I said, "somebody did it for him, somebody who could get out and come back in."

"I didn't see any tracks."

"You didn't look close enough. There were tracks, most of them wiped out and with leaves scattered over. Back in the brush a few steps I found some—woman's tracks."

"That sounds like Logan. He never got himself in trouble yet there wasn't some woman tryin' to get him out of it."

There was grass enough to keep the cattle happy, and we settled down to study what lay ahead of us. During the night, there could well be an attack. We had been warned in about the worst way, and we knew they would not hesitate to kill. The worst of it was that we did not know what was at stake except that Logan Sackett was somehow involved.

My night horse was fresh, and I shifted the saddle. Right now I wasn't sure whether I'd ride or walk, and I was thinking the last way might be best. Usually, I carried some moccasins in my outfit, and they were handy today.

Tyrel and Orrin stood with me at the last. "We'll handle things here. If there's shootin', don't worry yourself. We'll hold the fort."

Baptiste came to me. "A long time back there is a path down the mountain." He drew it in the dust. "The old fort is gone—only some stones here. This is grass. There is the river. I do not know what is here.

"The smokes—is ver' much smoke. Two, three fires, maybe." He hesitated. "A man who was at the fort, he tell me they find gold. Maybe—"

That could be the answer. But why threaten Logan with hanging? Why did he need cattle? Who was trying to prevent our arrival?

When darkness came, there were stars over the Cassiar Mountains, and I found Baptiste's trail and went down quietly to the water and crossed to the point where the old fort had stood. Some of the snow had melted, but there were patches which I avoided, not wanting to outline myself against the white or to leave tracks that could be found.

A straight dark line against the sky told me a building was there.

Where would Logan be? If I could find Logan, he could explain it all. Slowly, taking infinite care, I circled the area at the edge of the woods. I found a sluice, heard a rustle of running water in it. Somebody had been placering for gold.

A tent, and another tent. A canvas-walled house, a shedlike place, a log cabin with light shining from some cracks. A dug-out door with a bar across the outside—the *outside?*

For a moment, I held still in the shadows. Now why a bar across a door from the outside? Obviously not to keep anybody from getting in, so it must be to keep somebody from getting out.

Logan?

Maybe. There was a larger log cabin close by and light from a window made of old bottles, a window I could not see in, and nobody inside could see out. Beyond it, there was a corral. Easing along in the shadows, I counted at least twelve horses, and there were probably more.

There was a building with a porch in front of it, steps leading up to the door, and no light at all. It could be a store. In all, there were not more than five or six structures and a scattering of tents and lean-tos.

Nobody was moving around, and there seemed to be no dogs, or my presence would have been discovered. A door of a cabin opened, and a woman stood revealed in the door, a light behind her. She stood there for several minutes, and the night wind stirred her skirt. She brushed back a wisp of hair and went back inside, leaving the door open.

There was a fireplace in view, a homemade chair, a table, and some firewood piled by the fireplace. Suddenly, she came to the door again singing softly, "Bold, brave and undaunted . . ."

"Rode young Brennan on the moor!" I finished the line for her.

She ceased singing, swept off the door step, and then she spoke softly. "I shall lower the light and leave the door ajar."

She took a few more brushes with the broom, then stepped back inside and partly closed the door; then she lowered the light.

I hesitated. It might be a trap, but "Brennan on the Moor," about an Irish highwayman, was a favorite song of Logan's, and mine, for that matter.

I crossed the open space swiftly, flattened against the wall of the cabin to look and listen; then, silent as a ghost, I slipped inside.

She was waiting for me, her back to the table, her eyes wide. A surprisingly pretty girl with a firm chin and a straight, honest look to her.

"You will be William Tell," she said.

"I am."

"He described you to me, and Tyrel and Orrin as well. Even Lando, for we did not know who would come. He promised me that somebody would. I could not believe it."

"Three of us came, with some friends."

"I heard." There was something ironic in her voice. "I heard that you did not come alone."

"There's a girl with us who is looking for her brother, Douglas Molrone."

"He is here."

"Here?"

"Of course."

"And Logan?"

"He's here. He's getting over a broken leg. It should be almost healed by now, but I think he's prolonging it."

"If you are his nurse, I can understand why."

"He has no nurse. They permit no one near him."

"Who," I asked, "are 'they'?"

"There's gold here. Quite a lot of it, we believe. Some of us began finding it, first just a little, then more. We built a cabin or two and settled down to work.

"Then those others came. They saw what we were doing, and then they began to go to the store for supplies. At first, they bought a little as we did, then they returned for more. Nobody thought anything of it until my father went in to the store and found they had sold out. Everything was gone.

"John Fentrel, the storekeeper, sent a man out for supplies. He did not return.

"Then Logan Sackett came along. He came down the river in a canoe and tried to buy supplies at the store. Then he tried to buy from us, but we were down to almost nothing.

"He found out what had happened, and he offered to drive in a herd of beef cattle for us. He collected money from us, all we had. We managed to kill a little game, and we waited.

"Apparently, he had known of a small herd that had been driven part way here. Actually, I think the drover was headed for Barkerville and got hung up somewhere inland.

"Logan said he bought the herd from him and started back here. His men deserted him, but he kept on; then his cattle were stampeded, and his leg was broken."

"We got word somebody wanted to hang him."

"Some of us did. We thought he had taken our money and tried to get away with it. Some of us did not believe there had ever been any herd. Some of us thought he had lied. He promised us that if he could get a message out, he'd get cattle here before snow fell. There wasn't much else we could do, so we sent his message, and we've waited."

"Did you believe him?"

"Sort of. We sent a man out for supplies, and he got back, traveling at night with a canoe. He was going again, but his canoe was stolen.

"All the time those other men just loafed around, eating very well and just waiting. They mined very little and cut just enough wood for themselves and waited for us to starve.

"The man they called Cougar taunted us. He said if we were smart, we'd get out while we could, that Logan had lied and there was no herd. He said even if there was, there was no way cattle could reach us.

"They brought in more supplies, but they would sell none of them, and every man we sent out either failed to come back or had his supplies stolen.

"They wanted the gold for themselves, all of it, and they were trying to force us out. We put some fish traps in the river, Indian style, and that helped until they discovered what we were doing. They destroyed our traps as fast as we built them."

"How many of you are there?"

"Eight. There are four men and three women." She paused. "And there's a boy. Danny is about ten."

"And them?"

"There was just five of them. Now there are at least a dozen. Two of them were gone for quite a while, and when they came back, there were some other men with them. The two who left were George and Perry Stamper."

"We've met them."

He was listening. Several times he thought he heard faint sounds outside. He glanced at her. How far could he trust her? Was she one of *them?*

"Can you put names to the others?" he asked.

"Shanty's their leader, or he seems to be. That's Shanty Gavin. Then there's Doug Molrone—"

"He's one of them?"

"Yes, he is. He was one of the first ones. He came in with Shanty and the Stampers and that man Cougar. Oh, it's simple enough! If we leave, they will simply take over all the claims and have the gold to themselves! All they want to do is starve us out so we have to leave. Then they can say we abandoned the claims."

"Mind sitting in the dark?"

"What? Oh? No, not really. If you mean am I afraid of you, I'm not. Not in the least. I'm not afraid of any man."

"Put the light out, will you? There'll be the glow from the fireplace."

She glanced at me, then blew out the light. "Did you hear something?"

"I thought I did."

The fire had died to red coals. I liked the glow of it on her face. Her hair was dark, as were her eyes, and her skin deeply tanned.

"Where is your father?"

"He went away. He went overland to try to find supplies. He has not returned."

"You know who I am," I suggested.

She hesitated, then turned her eyes to me. "I am Laurie Gavin," she said.

189

Chapter XXV

"Gavin?"

"Shanty is my stepbrother," she explained.

"And Kyle?"

Surprised, she looked around at me. "What do you know of Kyle? But how could you know him? He is in Toronto!"

"He is on his way here, I believe."

"Kyle is my brother. My real brother."

I drew my gun. "Someone is coming, I think. Are you afraid?"

"Of course. I know them. On the surface, they are very quiet, very smooth, very soft-spoken, but do not trust them, William Tell Sackett, for they lie, and they will kill."

"Shanty, too?"

"He is the worst of them. Remember this. He is no blood brother of mine. My father married his mother, and he took our name. He preferred it to Stamper."

I returned the gun to its holster. There was a tap on the door. She glanced at me, and I said, "Answer it."

She went to the door. "Yes?" she said.

"Open the door, Laurie. You've a man in there we want."

She opened it, and Cougar and another, larger, more powerful man with a shock of blond hair stepped in.

"I am Tell Sackett," I said. "Are you looking for me?"

Cougar stepped aside. "Be careful, Shanty. This one's tough."

"Knowing that," I said, "might save us all some trouble."

Shanty had a nice smile. "But we've got you," he said. "There's no way you can get away."

I smiled back at him. "Then take me," I said. "I'm here."

Shanty hesitated. It worried him that I was not afraid, and he was a cautious man. I did not doubt his courage, but there is a time to be brave and a time not to be a damned fool.

"We've got your brother," he said. "We can kill him whenever we wish."

"Logan? He's not my brother, just a sort of distant cousin, but there are a lot of Sacketts, Shanty. If you step on the toes of one, they all come running."

"You came," he admitted. "I never thought you'd make it."

"There are two more up on the mountain, and by now they're beginning to miss me. They're getting lonely on the mountain, Shanty, and they'll come down."

"We will handle them."

"And there are more of us where we came from. Be smart, Shanty. Cash in your chips while you still can. Walk away from here now. Just lay down your hand."

He laughed, and there was real humor in it. "You know, Sackett, I like you. I'm going to hate to kill you."

"We've brought the cattle through, Shanty. In spite of all your boys could do, they are here. There's beef enough to last the winter through, and we might get in some other supplies before the cold sets in.

"As far as that goes, we can let them have what's left of our supplies. You played a strong hand, but when the showdown came, you just didn't have it."

Out on the mountain, I head a wild, clear yell in the night, and I knew what it was. The boys were bringing the cattle down. They'd be here soon; no doubt some of them already were.

"He's right." It was a voice behind me, a voice I

191

knew. It was Logan. He appeared from behind the curtain covering the door to Laurie's bedroom.

"Sorry, Laurie, but I had to use your window. It isn't quite shut."

Shanty looked from one to the other. "He's yours, Cougar. You always thought you could take him."

Logan was leaning on a crutch, but suddenly he dropped it and stood on his two feet. "That bar of yours," he said, "I just poked a stick through a crack and worked it loose. I tried it a week ago and found it would work." He smiled. "I was waitin' for the Sacketts. I knew they'd come. They always come."

Laurie stepped back.

Shanty's expression had changed. The humor was gone now. His eyes were large. I knew he was ready. I knew he was a dangerous man. Cougar had eyes only for Logan, who was smiling widely.

Outside in the town, I could hear the stir of cattle, a rattle of spurs on the porch of the store.

Then I heard Orrin speak. "Up to you, George. You and Perry can take a canoe and go down river. There's lots of new country waiting." He paused. "All your boys can just ride out, walk out, or paddle out, but all of you are leaving."

It was quiet in the room where we stood. We were listening.

"Not Doug!" That was Nettie. "He's my brother! He wouldn't—"

"He did," somebody else said. "He was one of the worst of them. Some men will do anything for gold."

"Not Doug!" she protested.

"I was in it, Sis. I was in it all the way! It was a chance to get rich! To get rich all at once! To get rich without all that slavin', standing in icy water, panning out gold! I could sell the claim! I could—!"

"And now you can't," Tyrel said.

"It was worth a try," Shanty said, and went for his gun.

Only the red glow of the fire, then a moment of

crashing thunder, the brief stabs of gun lightning in the half light.

Outside in the street, the sound was echoed. There was a sound of running, a scream, a pound of racing hoofs.

Tell and Logan Sackett stood alone in the red glow from the fire. Behind them, on the edge of a bench, Laurie sat, horror stricken, gripped fast in shock.

Shanty Gavin stared up at them. "Damn it! Damn it to hell! It looked so good! We had it all! They'd starve out and pull out, and we'd work and then sell! It was a cinch! We had a pat hand!"

Me, I was reloading my gun, and Logan looked down at him. "You had a pat hand, all right, Shanty. You've still got it. Five of a kind, right in the belly!"

Laurie stood up. "Tell—please! Take me out of here."

"We can go out the easier way," Logan said, "down to the Stikine River and out to Wrangell and the sea. Then a ship to Frisco."

Cap looked over at Mary McCann. "If this was where you was comin', you got here too late. You want to go out with me?"

Nettie was standing there alone, and Orrin went to her.

"He ran," she said. "Doug ran away."

"The Stampers didn't," Tyrel said, "and look where they are."

"It's getting light," Orrin said. "What's the matter with this country?"

"That's because it's morning," Tyrel said. "The sun's comin' up."

"Mr. Sackett?" It was John Fentrell. "This may seem a bad time and all, but with you and your boys talking of leaving, I think you should come into the store and we'll settle up."

Laurie was walking down toward the gravel point where the old landing had been. "I'll be along," I said, and went inside.

Fentrell looked old and tired He removed a loose board and lifted out some sacks of gold "If they knew where it was," he said "They'd have taken it all."

The gold was there on the counter. It was not enough but it was all they had. We would have debts to pay and hard work to do to make up for the time.

So I taken the gold and walked outside into the morning sun and looked toward the shore where the rest of them had gathered by the boats.

"Mr. Fentrell," I said "we left one man up yonder." I gestured toward the trail down which we had come. "Walk up there and see him sometime."

Shorty was a good man, and he'd come a far piece, and I hoped he wouldn't be lonely on the mountain.

ABOUT LOUIS L'AMOUR

"I think of myself in the oral tradition—as a troubadour, a village taleteller, the man in the shadows of the campfire. That's the way I'd like to be remembered—as a storyteller. A good storyteller."

It is doubtful that any author could be as at home in the world recreated in his novels as Louis Dearborn L'Amour. Not only could he physically fill the boots of the rugged characters he writes about, but he has literally "walked the land my characters walk." His personal experiences as well as his lifelong devotion to historical research have combined to give Mr. L'Amour the unique knowledge and understanding of the people, events, and challenge of the American frontier that have become the hallmarks of his popularity.

Of French-Irish descent, Mr. L'Amour can trace his own family in North America back to the early 1600s and follow their steady progression westward, "always on the frontier." As a boy growing up in Jamestown, North Dakota, he absorbed all he could about his family's frontier heritage, including the story of his great-grandfather who was scalped by Sioux warriors.

Spurred by an eager curiosity and desire to broaden his horizons, Mr. L'Amour left home at the age of fifteen and enjoyed a wide variety of jobs including seaman, lumberjack, elephant handler, skinner of dead cattle, assessment miner, and officer on tank destroyers during World War II. During his "yondering" days he also circled the world on a freighter, sailed a dhow on the Red Sea, was shipwrecked in the West Indies and stranded in the Mojave Desert. He has won fifty-one of fifty-nine fights as a professional boxer and worked as a journalist and lecturer. A voracious reader and collector of rare books, Mr. L'Amour's personal library of some 10,000 volumes covers a broad range of scholarly disciplines including many personal papers, maps, and diaries of the pioneers.

Mr. L'Amour "wanted to write almost from the time I could walk." After developing a widespread following for his many adventure stories written for the fiction magazines, Mr. L'Amour published his first full-length novel, *Hondo*, in 1953. Mr. L'Amour is now one of the four bestselling living novelists in the world. Every one of his more than 85 novels is constantly in print and every one has sold more than one million copies, giving him more million-copy bestsellers than any other living author. His books have been translated into more than a dozen languages, and more than thirty of his novels and stories have been made into feature films and television movies.

Among Mr. L'Amour's most popular books are *The Lonesome Gods, Comstock Lode, The Cherokee Trail, Flint, Son of a Wanted Man, The Shadow Riders, Silver Canyon, Bowdrie, The Walking Drum*, his historical novel of the 12th century, and his series of novels which tells the continuing saga of the Sackett family, the latest of which is the bestseller *Jubal Sackett*.

The recipient of many great honors and awards, in 1983 Mr. L'Amour became the first novelist ever to be awarded a Special National Gold Medal by the United States Congress in honor of his life's work. In 1984 he was also awarded the Medal of Freedom by President Ronald Reagan.

Mr. L'Amour lives in Los Angeles with his wife, Kathy, and their two children, Beau and Angelique.

Special Offer
Buy a Bantam Book
for only 50¢.

Now you can have an up-to-date listing of Bantam's hundreds of titles plus take advantage of our unique and exciting bonus book offer. A special offer which gives you the opportunity to purchase a Bantam book for only 50¢. Here's how!

By ordering any five books at the regular price per order, you can also choose any other single book listed (up to a $4.95 value) for just 50¢. Some restrictions do apply, but for further details why not send for Bantam's listing of titles today!

Just send us your name and address and we will send you a catalog!